CW00664613

Levi: Driverton 2

The Barrington Billionaires

Book 14

Ruth Cardello

Author Contact

website: RuthCardello.com
email: rcardello@ruthcardello.com
Facebook: Author Ruth Cardello
Twitter: RuthieCardello

Copyright

Levi: Driverton 2
Copyright © 2024 by Ruth Cardello
Print Edition

ISBN eBook: 978-1-951888-75-6
ISBN Print: 978-1-951888-76-3

An Original work by Ruth Cardello

Driverton's bad boy is falling in love with his best friend's cousin and it just might cost him everything.

Levi has always had a sweet spot for Katie, but she's not his type. He likes his women wild, willing, and from out of town so they're easy to move on from when his interest wanes.

Katie is opinionated and off-limits. She's also so damn loyal he'd tear out his own heart before risking breaking hers.

Things begin to heat up when, side by side, they train to become part of an organization that rescues runaways and kidnapped children. He's always known he's not the right man for her, but he had no idea how hard it would be to refuse her when they begin to share the same goals and dreams.

One night of weakness could cost him everyone he cares about—including her.

Dedication

This book is dedicated to all the people who live with questions they aren't sure they want the answers to. I hope they one day find peace in either knowing or letting the questions go.

Prologue

O N A PRIVATE jet heading west across the US, Bradford Wilson scanned a briefing on an open missing person's case. The son of a senator had been last seen heli-skiing in Alaska. An extensive search for him had ended without success. His skis had been found halfway down the mountain, but there was no sign of him. It wasn't the type of job Bradford usually considered, but the senator had powerful friends who'd sought the resources of not only government agencies but Ian Barrington. Ian and Bradford had a long history and, regardless of the financial cost or legality of the request, they were each other's one-ring pick up.

Having grown up in the world of the elite, Ian was smooth and diplomatic with get-out-of-jail connections all over the world. Hardened from a much different upbringing, Bradford was better at intimidation and termination. As a team they were formidable.

Cellphone records showed the teen's phone had been turned on one time since he'd gone missing and had connected to a tower briefly in Utah before being turned off again. The senator had recently taken a controversial stance against defense contracts being awarded to international companies, one of which was based in Utah. It was suspected that the senator's son was being used as leverage to sway his vote and that the phone had been turned on strategically as a warning. No calls had been made since. No charges to a credit card. No facial recognition hits on any of the government surveillance databases. Whoever had taken the kid was good at covering their tracks. It had the potential of being a high-profile situation that needed to be dealt with swiftly, deadly, and with untraceable precision.

When Bradford's phone beeped with an incoming call, he checked it and nearly let it go to voicemail, but since his wife, Joanna, had asked him to be nicer to Clay Landon, he felt obligated to answer. "What do you need Clay?"

"I have a dilemma I'd like your opinion on."

"Is Boppy messing in the house again?" He asked about Clay's tiny dog with more sarcasm than he should have, but he and Clay had zero common experience. Clay had been born with more money than God and considered needing to shop for something himself a crisis. Bradford had survived poverty as well as gang violence as a child and bore the physical scars on both his face and body as a reminder.

They were not the same.

"No, her sitter resolved that, but thanks for asking. It was a problem for a while."

"Glad to hear it." Bradford sighed. There was a good

chance Clay's only reason for calling was that he was bored again. Experience with people of extreme wealth had convinced Bradford that limitless resources were detrimental to a person's instincts for self-preservation as well as their social intelligence. When a person could have whatever they wanted whenever they wanted it, their life lacked struggle and strife, so they created it.

Like heli-skiing alone without security or cell service.

I'll never understand people.

As Joanna had reminded Bradford more than once, Clay wasn't a bad person. In fact, he was generous to a fault when it came to helping causes or people. Where Joanna's and Bradford's opinion of Clay differed was when it came to the reasoning behind all that generosity. Joanna saw kindness and concern, whereas Bradford saw immature attempts to gain acceptance from his peers—people Bradford thought Clay should waste less time trying to impress.

Like me.

Clay sounded more serious than usual when he spoke. "The best thing you ever did for me was locating Cooper. I don't know if I could have found him without you."

That sounded oddly humble for Clay. "I appreciate that, thank you."

"So, in the spirit of that, I tracked down Levi's parents."

"You did what?"

"I found them."

"Where?"

"On a private island about sixty miles off the coast of

3

Florida. Trust me, it wasn't easy. I had to go back a decade and retrace their journey from New England down the East Coast. I almost gave up; the reports were so sad in the beginning. But I asked myself what you would do, and I kept my private detectives on the trail."

That was actually impressive for him. "What's the dilemma? Are you not sure if you should tell Levi? I would. He deserves to know."

"They're not the people they were when they left Driverton . . ."

"Doesn't matter. Tell Levi you found them and the ball is in his court as far as how much he wants to know or if he wants to contact them."

"I flew down to check out their situation and it was a very *revealing* one."

"What are you talking about, Clay?"

"Driverton, for all its strengths, is a bit of a sheltered place. There's also no such thing as a secret there. Levi's life has been tough enough. He might not need to know where they ended up."

"Oh, my God, Clay. Just say it. What did you find down in Florida?"

Chapter One

Katie

I USED TO think life got easier as you got older, but clearly that isn't the case.

Leaning on the fiberglass handles of a post hole digger, I wiped the back of one hand across my damp forehead. With the coming of fall, the temperature had already begun to dip in Maine. I was too distracted to enjoy the cool breeze.

A few feet away, my cousin Ollie muttered something as he deepened the last hole I'd dug, but my attention wasn't on him either. No, no matter how many times I told myself not to look, my gaze returned to our friend Levi as he hauled cement bags from the back of his truck to place them beside the holes we'd dug. I watched him toss a fresh bag of cement onto one shoulder, effortlessly carry it to where Ollie was working, then lay it beside the hole before returning with a heavy wooden post. Levi was tall and lean, but strong from a lifetime of working his small farm. His jeans were stained with grease and paint. His faded T-shirt had definitely seen better days, but its tight fit clung to his muscular back in the most distracting way. There likely wasn't a single woman in a hundred-mile radius who wouldn't have been flirting with him if she were in my place.

I forced myself to look away again because he and I could never be more than friends. Topping the list of why? How well I knew him. I'd grown up watching him break the heart of every woman he dated and make a fool of himself chasing the only one who'd turned him down—Mary. Even if I could put all that aside, he was Ollie's best friend and I never wanted to be the reason that changed. Levi had always been and would always be off-limits.

My gaze returned to him as he made another trip to his truck. No man had the right to look as good as he did in a pair of old jeans. *Damn.*

Despite his reputation with women, Levi had never been anything but wonderful to me. Maybe because he didn't have a sister to look after, he'd watched out for me. He was the one who'd taught me to double-knot my shoelaces so I'd stop tripping over them. When both my brother, Tom, and Ollie had become impatient with my reluctance to remove the training wheels from my bike, it had been Levi who'd held the back of it and encouraged me until I'd sped off on my own.

It felt wrong to see him as anything but someone who'd always been kind to me. When he'd found himself suddenly alone in high school, Aunt Reana had rallied friends and neighbors to support him as he became the man of the house his parents had walked away from.

"Back to work," Ollie said with the same voice of authority he used when I lingered on break while working for him at his restaurant, Little Willie's.

I shot him a side-eye warning but lifted the hole digger again. "You realize I've dug more holes than you have today."

"I'd be digging my own if I didn't have to finish all of yours," Ollie said without missing a beat. He was being an ass because he didn't want to be there, and it was beginning to get on my last nerve.

I held out the digger toward him. "Okay. Show me how it's done."

From the corner of my eye, I caught Levi returning with several posts stacked on one shoulder. "You tell him, Katie. Or if he wants, he can take this job." The smile he flashed sent a flush of warmth through me. It wasn't difficult to understand why so many women took a chance on him despite his reputation for loving and leaving. He had the bad boy, I-dare-you-to-try-to-redeem-me persona down to an art. It wasn't an act. Whenever he and Ollie headed off somewhere together, Aunt Reana said a prayer aloud for their "damn fool souls." Together, they'd made their fair share of poor choices. If the three of us hadn't agreed to train with Bradford, Ollie and Levi would already be downing the lunchtime beers I'd reluctantly be serving them.

It wasn't that I'd done much better with my own life, but I was trying to turn that around. Really, really trying.

I bit my bottom lip as Levi bent to gently lay the wood posts in a pile near us. He was already strong. How would he look after weeks of physical training with Bradford? For the sake of the local women, I hoped not too much better.

"I'm done," Ollie said. "We could have finished hours ago. Levi, go get your auger."

"No." Levi placed another post beside a bag of cement before answering him. "This isn't about convenience."

"Right. It's a punishment," Ollie growled. "Meant to humble us."

I inhaled sharply. "It's not like we don't deserve it. Bradford didn't ask us for anything the first time."

Ollie snorted. "Deserve it? We saved a woman's life. How does that equate to us becoming Bradford's free labor?"

Levi ran a hand through his hair. "Are we doing this, or not? We agreed to take the training seriously this time. If we're just going to fuck around, I have shit to do back at my place."

"No," the word was wrenched out of me with such emotion both of them turned to me with concern. "You will *not* take this opportunity from me again. I want to learn everything Bradford has to teach us. I intend to be strong, skilled, and capable of making a real difference. If either of you ruin this for me—"

"Hey," Levi said gently. "No one is going to ruin anything for you."

"No one made you quit with us the first time," Ollie pointed out.

My temper flared. "I was scared. I didn't think I could do it without you, but I'd probably be better off alone. Fine. Go. I don't need your negativity."

"You think you're such a ray of sunshine?" Ollie slammed the blade of his shovel into the earth. "I'm getting tired of you lecturing me like you've lived this perfect life while I've been—"

"Breaktime," Levi announced. "Who's hungry? I picked up sandwiches from Manju's. They're in my truck. Why don't you go get them, Ollie?"

Ollie grumbled, "I'm not hungry. It's not even eleven."

Levi continued, "Go get the fucking sandwiches, Ollie. Use the walk to remember how much you love Katie, then come back and apologize."

"For not enjoying putting in a fence in the least time-effective way possible?"

I folded my arms in front of me. Sobriety was turning my usually easy-going cousin into a real asshole.

Levi held Ollie's gaze. "You said you'd take it seriously this time."

Ollie threw his hands up in the air. "Of course you side with her."

Levi's attention turned to me. "When he apologizes to you, say something nice to him. We're just as scared as you are that we won't pass Bradford's tests."

Ollie snarled, "I'm not—"

"You're afraid too?" *Levi?* I didn't know he was afraid of anything.

Levi shrugged. "Of course I am. It's a big deal. It could change all of our lives. I know that. Ollie does too." He leaned in close enough that I flushed. "And neither of us is going to let you or ourselves down this time. We're in this together. When one of us stumbles, we reach down, haul their ass up, and keep going. Deal?"

I swallowed hard, doing my best to remember all the reasons he would be bad for me. "Deal," I whispered.

He raised his head and nodded toward Ollie. "Deal?"

"I never said I was quitting." Ollie grumbled. "And Katie knows I love her."

I tore my attention from Levi to meet my cousin's gaze. "I love you too."

Ollie cleared his throat. "I know how important this is, Katie. I won't let you down."

It was such a sweet softening, I said, "I don't mean to lecture you. I do that when I worry about you, Levi . . . and me."

"I know," Ollie said. "It's fucking annoying, but since you're family . . ." He followed those words with a smile.

"Go get the damn sandwiches," I said with a laugh of relief.

Left alone for a moment, Levi and I fell into an awkward

silence. I wasn't used to things between us being strained, but lately they definitely were. In a quiet tone, Levi said, "I'm not going anywhere. I'm all in. We're going to do this, Katie—together."

I wondered how many women wished he'd said those words to them. The irony wasn't lost on me. The reason he could easily proclaim his loyalty to me was because he didn't see me as a woman. In his eyes, I would probably always be the little girl he'd taught to play chess because our high school had scholarships for being on the team and I'd dreamed of leaving Driverton to attend college.

Not that I'd gone. No, I'd made plenty of bad choices as well. Together, though, we were vowing to leave all that behind. "Thank you." I placed a hand on his arm. "I need this."

"We all do." He laid his hand over mine. "And never apologize for caring so much. It's part of what I've always found beautiful about you."

He stepped back and walked after Ollie.

I stood there watching him go.

Beautiful? Me? Was that how he saw me?

Was it how I wanted him to?

Chapter Two

Levi

I NEED TO stop saying shit like that to Katie.

With everything that had been going on in Driverton, I hadn't left town to forage for female companionship in a while. Too long, apparently. I needed to remedy that before I did something stupid like forget why I could never see Katie as anything more than a little sister.

Katie was one hundred percent off limits.

Period.

I glanced back at her. She smiled and my heart thudded in my chest before I turned away again. A man knows when a woman is interested and there was no denying the long looks Katie had been giving me lately. More times than I cared to admit, I'd been accused of being cold-hearted, emotionally unavailable . . . immature . . . stunted. Women threw a lot of nasty labels my way when things ended, but what they couldn't call me was a liar. I didn't lead them on with promises of more than a good time. There'd only ever been one woman I'd offered more to. Looking back, I'm not entirely sure why I'd ever thought Mary and I belonged together. She was innocent while I was running wild. Her parents protected and adored her. Mine had chosen each other and whatever the hell they'd found outside of Driverton over me. Maybe it was because her life had seemed so perfect, and I'd wanted a little of that for myself.

Whatever the reason, getting stoned and accidentally proposing to her mother instead of her had cemented my bad reputation and removed any chance I'd had of winning her heart. Ollie said it was a delib-cident: an accident a person does deliberately to get out of doing something they know they shouldn't

No one knew me better than Ollie, so I didn't say he was wrong. I wasn't the right man for Mary, just like I could never be the right man for Katie. I didn't see myself as a bad person or a bad friend. Sure, I'd caused my share of trouble in Driverton over the years, but show me a person who says there's nothing they regret and I'll show you a damn liar.

It was only when it came to romantic relationships and considering forever with someone that I had no fucks to give. Not one. I'd lost count of the number of women I'd dated, definitely had sex with more than my fair share, and didn't care if I saw any of them again. Sex was fun. I cared enough about whoever I was with to make it as good for them as it was for me, but something shut down in me as soon as they started to get emotionally attached. As long as I was clear about that from the start, I didn't see anything wrong with what I was doing. Hell, most of the time I wasn't the one suggesting we take things to the bedroom . . . or the backseat of a car . . . or an empty stairwell.

Women saw me as a challenge. Or, like me, they weren't looking for more than a fun fuck. I don't claim to understand the inner workings of a woman's mind. I was clear about what I was willing to offer and let them decide if they wanted to be with me or not. Some women thought they could change me.

None had even come close.

Looking back, I was pretty sure Mary wouldn't have either. Was that why I'd screwed that up as royally as I had? An innocent like her would have been crushed when I moved on . . . and I would have.

I could never do that to Mary.

And I couldn't do it to Katie either.

Ollie was muttering something to himself when I joined him at my truck. "Hey, you okay?"

He turned, sandwiches in hand, and met my gaze. "I drank last night. After I closed Little Willie's. I stayed, sat at the bar, and did shots . . ."

I leaned back against the truck. "Okay."

"Half a bottle. All by myself."

I folded my arms across my chest and sighed. We were quickly entering uncomfortable territory. It was disappointing to hear that he'd broken our pact to stay sober during training, but I was far from someone who could judge anyone.

He continued, "Like someone with a fucking drinking problem."

I nodded.

"I'm pissed at myself."

"Yep."

"And at you and Katie for deciding we weren't good enough as we were."

"I understand." I didn't, not really, but that wasn't what he needed to hear.

"I feel like shit today."

I nodded again. What could I say to that?

He added, "How could you stop cold turkey? Aren't you craving it? I feel like I'm fighting a demon and losing to it."

He was and it wasn't fair. Life wasn't fair. I'd learned that early enough. I would have given Ollie one of my organs if that's what he needed, but I didn't know what to give him to help him with this. "There must be an Alcoholics Anonymous or something like that in a town nearby. I can help you find one."

"I don't want anyone to know." Emotion shone in his eyes and clogged my throat.

There were no secrets in Driverton, but I understood when a person had nothing else their pride mattered even more. "Do you trust me?"

"You know I do."

"Give me a day and I'll come back to you with a solution."

He looked down at the sandwiches he'd crushed in his hands. "I don't expect you to solve this. I just needed to say it out loud to someone I knew wouldn't judge me." He glanced over to Katie. "You know what you said earlier about being afraid? I am. But not afraid of failing myself. I don't want to fail my family. Katie deserves better than this. My mom does as well. I know I haven't been a stellar son or cousin, but when we were all fucking up together, I didn't feel . . ."

"I get it. We all felt trapped here and surviving was success. But now we're being offered a chance to be more and that's fucking terrifying."

Ollie laughed without humor. "You do understand."

After a pause, I said, "I can't go back, Ollie. We had a lot of fun together, but even if we could turn back time and not have Cooper's family find him . . . never meet everyone he brought to Driverton . . . I wouldn't want to. We have a chance to be part of something important and to make a real difference." I glanced over at Katie. "And we have people counting on us."

"I know." His fist hitting the side of my truck brought my attention back to him. "What if I can't beat this?"

"You can. You will. Last night you stumbled. We've all been there. But you're not alone. I've got you. We'll get through this."

He nodded, then rubbed the back of his neck with one hand. "I've been snapping at Katie all day. She does deserve an apology."

"Yes, she does."

He looked down at the misshapen sandwiches again. "This is a poor peace offering."

I met Katie's concerned gaze across the distance. "I'm sure she'll accept it. I'll give you a few minutes to talk it out."

Ollie socked my shoulder with a punch. "Thanks."

I pretended it hurt and hit him back. "You're welcome."

He'd just rejoined Katie when a truck pulled up beside mine. Bradford. It wasn't good timing for him to check up on us.

"Lunch break already?" Bradford asked in a tone thick with sarcasm as he joined me. He was a large man, taller than most, and built square and muscled like a pit bull. His face and body were scarred from horrors that he'd shared glimpses of on the rare occasions when he'd over-indulged on moonshine with us.

He was a hard-ass, a badass, and had probably killed as many people as I'd fucked, but in my eyes, he was a hero. Although done differently, he and Cooper had both made it their personal mission to locate and rescue missing children. Together they were establishing headquarters for that kind of work right here in Driverton. If Ollie, Katie, and I passed Bradford's training program, we would join their organization and be a part of something so important its existence could never be spoken of to anyone outside of it. Sometimes the whole situation still felt a bit unreal, but it was happening.

I took a deep breath and chose my words carefully. "Bradford, I need your help."

Bradford's only response was a narrowing of his eyes and a nod.

"I want to send Ollie to a rehab center without anyone knowing, so I need you to say you're sending him for special spy training."

With a disgusted grunt, Bradford asked, "He's drinking again?"

I rose to my full height and turned to face him. He was an inch or two taller and more muscled, but I'd always been a hard one to intimidate. "He's struggling. I'm going to do this with or without you. I'm not asking you for money, just a cover story."

"Rehab centers are expensive."

"I have savings and if it's more than that . . . I'll find the money. I don't care if I have to sell my truck."

For a long moment, Bradford seemed to weigh my words. "Clay is installing high-tech equipment beneath the police station that someone will need to learn how to use."

"Ollie's always been good with computers. It would be awesome if he could come home with more than just sobriety. I'll find a rehab center, then we could coordinate something."

"I'll arrange both. I have friends in Boston who know how to bring out the best in people. I'll set him up near them. They'll check on him. I also know people who will send him back knowing more about Clay's computer systems than Clay ever will."

I almost said that wouldn't be hard, but Clay was growing on me. He meant well. Instead, I relaxed my stance and joked, "You have friends outside of Driverton?"

"Fuck you." He smiled.

I returned the smile, then sobered. "He's struggling, Bradford. Whatever this costs, I'll make it happen."

"No need." His eyes darkened. "Isn't this what friends do for each other?"

I nodded. It was odd that a man the CIA considered one of their deadliest weapons was just as broken on the inside as the rest of us. He'd come to Driverton to find Cooper Landon but had stayed when he'd seen how the people in this small town watched out for each other. He and Joanna were part of our community now and he was right that this was the kind of thing we did for each other. I decided to lighten the mood, so I asked, "Do friends make friends dig fence holes all day?"

He smiled at that. "They do. They also plan afternoons that involve running until you vomit, lifting weights until your arms shake, and learning how to take a punch without crying."

I laughed even though I wasn't sure he was joking. "We

must be besties because that sounds perfect."

He scanned the area. "You're done for today. Clean up and have everyone meet me at the house."

I nodded. "Bradford."

His attention returned to me.

I said, "Ollie's trying this time." Bradford gave me a long look I wasn't sure how to interpret. He wouldn't be there if he didn't care. Still, I felt there was something I needed to say. "If it were you or me struggling, he'd make sure we got what we needed. I don't know where I would have ended up if he and his family hadn't stepped up to help me when my parents tapped out. The Williams are good people, but they don't take help easily. We need to do this in a way that leaves them with their pride."

"Understood." After a moment, he added. "You'll be one man down tomorrow and the fence is a big job. I'll hire someone to complete it."

Flexing my shoulders back, I shook my head. "No need. We can finish it."

He cocked an eyebrow.

I added, "Training with you is important to Katie. She'll feel like we failed our first task if we don't complete the fence."

Eyes narrowing, Bradford looked from me to where Katie and Ollie were putting cement around a post. "Ollie is lucky to have you as a friend."

"He's family."

"Family." Bradford echoed the word slowly. "Do you ever wonder where your parents are?"

"I do not," I bit out.

"If you ever did—"

"No offense, Bradford, but I'd rather talk about people who actually matter to me."

He nodded toward Ollie. "Then all I have to say is don't betray Ollie's trust while he's gone."

My head snapped back. I had no idea what he was referring to—until I did, and heat rose up the back of my neck.

He turned and walked away while I was still choking on my declaration that there was zero possibility of that happening. Katie met my gaze, this time with a question in her eyes. She wanted to know what Bradford and I had discussed. I'd tell her it was none of her business, but she'd never accept that answer.

I'd have to lie.

I'd never done that with her before. Katie was one of a handful of people I would do nearly anything to not disappoint. In my heart, she was family as well—family that lately made the air sizzle and my dick swell when she looked at me with longing in her eyes.

It needed to stop. I was a grown man, not a teenager at the mercy of my raging hormones. I looked away and groaned as I realized for Bradford to issue the warning he had, I must have been just as guilty of sending the wrong message as she was.

No, Katie.

It doesn't matter that your body might fit perfectly with mine.

We can never happen.

Chapter Three

Katie

I WAS AT Ollie's side as he met Levi halfway to his truck. "What did Bradford want?" Ollie asked in a tight tone.

The pause before Levi answered was all I needed to know that his next words would be a lie. I'd known him my whole life. Did he think I hadn't seen him pause that exact same way when my aunt used to ask him how things were with his mother, and he told her they were fine?

I just never thought he'd lie to Ollie *or me*.

I held my breath and clung to my faith in him. Levi knew how important working with Bradford was to me. He wouldn't let me down.

The strained smile he shot both of us was another tell. He didn't want to say whatever he was about to. *Holy shit, what did you do, Levi?*

"He said there's an opportunity to learn about the computer systems Clay is installing beneath the station. Only one slot, though. I told him he should consider you, Ollie. He agreed that you're the best fit. You've always loved technology. Looks like you're going to Boston for a few weeks."

"*I* love computers," I said in a rush. Is that what Levi feels bad about? That he didn't even consider that I might want a chance at that training?

"You do." Ollie put a hand on my arm. "If there's only one slot, Katie should have it. She's smart. Look at how fast she taught herself to pick locks."

"No," Levi said firmly. "It's been decided. He's already setting everything up."

Ollie frowned. "I don't understand."

Arms folded across his chest, Levi said, "You said you trust me."

"You told him," Ollie growled.

"I'm sorry," I interjected. "What would Levi tell Bradford?"

Levi lowered his arms, but his jaw remained tight as he said, "You're going to Boston, Ollie. Most likely leaving tomorrow. You've been saying you want to learn a new skill, and this is your opportunity. If our roles were reversed, you'd make me go. Don't fuck this up."

Scanning both of their faces provided no clarification, so I asked, "Anyone want to tell me what's going on? Anyone?"

Crickets.

If I didn't credit myself with being too mature to, I would have stomped my feet and demanded they answer me. Part of me was still disappointed I wasn't given a chance at what sounded like a good opportunity, but Ollie did deserve it as much as I did. So, I just stood there, hands on my hips, waiting for one of them to acknowledge that I'd even spoken.

Ollie rubbed a hand over his face. "Will I actually come back trained to use Clay's system?"

"Bradford said you would, and he doesn't say anything he doesn't mean."

"Okay," Ollie said with a nod. The emotion I saw welling in his eyes robbed me of any irritation.

I looked quickly from Ollie to Levi and back. I would have bet my life Ollie was in some kind of trouble and Levi had found a way to help him. Neither wanted me to know. I nearly burst into tears at the beauty of it. If Levi hadn't slept with half the population of Maine, I would have fallen in love with him right then and there.

The silence that followed was strained until Levi said, "There'll be other opportunities, Katie."

Although I wished Levi felt he could tell me what was really going on, I wasn't surprised. My family was ripe with proud men who stubbornly thought women would think less of them if they admitted any weakness. They opened doors for us, carried whatever they deemed too heavy for us, and leapt into battle mode at the slightest hint that we might require their protection.

It was hard to hate them for that.

Their protective nature didn't stop with women. Ollie had never fought a fight that Levi wasn't willing to jump in to defend him. And the reverse was just as true. How that had never translated to Levi being with the same woman for more than a week was a mystery to me, but I knew it had to do with how he'd been left behind by his parents.

Levi had issues.

But so did I.

And, although they didn't want me to know, apparently so did Ollie.

I could have said I was onto them, but I chose the kinder path and pinned Levi with what I hoped was an annoyed look. "It would have been nice to have been asked."

The amount of charm in Levi's smile as he said, "You'll get over it," rocked me back onto my heels. When he winked, I swallowed hard then my lips parted as I sucked in a shaky breath.

Ollie chimed in. "When I get back, Katie, I'll make sure to teach you everything they showed me about the system."

I tore my gaze from Levi's to clear my head. Ollie had been a pill that day, but I knew how much he loved me and that made everything both easier and more complicated. "I know you will, Ollie. Thanks." A quick glance at Levi's face revealed he wasn't handling lying to me well. *Good.* "We should probably get back to work."

Levi said, "Bradford wants us to clean up and head to his house. Looks like we'll be going for a run, lifting weights, and learning some self-defense. I don't know for sure. When Everette worked with Bradford, it was intense."

My chin rose. "Bring it on. We can handle it."

Cocking his head to one side, Levi smirked, "You did hear me say *run*, right?"

Oh, was he starting shit with me? "I did." If he mentioned the twenty pounds I'd put on since high school, I'd kick his ass. "I don't need to keep up with Bradford, I just need to outpace you."

His mouth rounded. "You think you run faster than I do?"

I chuckled. "I know I can. I was on the track team in high school. When was the last time you ran anywhere?"

The world around us disappeared until there was nothing beyond that sexy smile of his and the twinkle in his eyes when he said, "There's more than one way to stay in shape."

Without missing a beat, I replied, "I don't believe three-second sprints, no matter how many you've had, could adequately prepare you to match my stamina." Realizing only after I'd said the words how they could be interpreted, I rushed to add, "At running."

"Levi," Ollie growled. "Go start your truck."

There was a sparkle in Levi's eyes as he held back whatever he was thinking. With a shake of his head, Levi tore his eyes from mine, then trotted off. Although he wasn't beefed up like Bradford, he was definitely physically fit. *Could* I outrun him?

Would any woman want to?

As soon as he was out of earshot, Ollie said, "Looks like I

might be going out of town for a bit."

I allowed myself to continue to appreciate the perfection of the backside of Levi as he made his way to his truck. "I know and don't feel bad about it. You deserve the chance as much as I do."

He cleared his throat. "You know I love Levi. He's the closest thing I have to a brother."

Without meeting his gaze, I shrugged. "I know."

"Please don't make me kill him."

My eyes flew to his. "What?"

He sighed. "Levi is an amazing friend. He'd take a bullet for either of us. But I see the way he looks at you lately."

Pleasure flooded through me even as I tried to keep my head. "He looks at every woman that way."

"Exactly. Remember that. Don't encourage him. You're the only thing I could imagine ending our friendship."

My mouth dropped open, and I gasped. "First of all, I'm not a thing. Second, you don't get to tell me who I can or can't be with."

Ollie raised both hands in surrender as he said, "We both know you haven't always had good judgment when it comes to men."

Family. They could take you from happy to homicidal with both skill and speed. "Ollie," I said between gritted teeth, "I was young and stupid when I left town with someone I shouldn't have. I don't deny that. But it was one time. I will not spend the rest of my life apologizing for it.

Take that back."

His chest puffed as he inhaled deeply. "Sorry."

"You should be. That was low."

Ollie hooked his thumbs into the front pockets of his jeans. "He'd break your heart, Katie, and not because he'd want to. It's just the way he is."

"Why do you talk about Levi like I don't know him?"

"Because you get all goofy around him lately. You're playing with fire. If you ever did hook up with him, when he broke it off, and he would, everything would change. I couldn't forgive him for hurting you. Aunt Reana couldn't either. If I didn't knock Levi into next week, your brother would risk his pension to. Once those dominoes start falling and people start taking sides there's a risk Levi could lose everything. Is that what you want?"

"Or, *hear me out*, we could all be adults about this and not think that everything that happens in Driverton is everyone's business."

Ollie made a frustrated sound. "I can't stop you. All I can do is caution you and hope you'll realize that you wouldn't be the only person hurt."

"I'm confused. Are you worried about me or Levi?"

"Both." He laid a hand on my shoulder. "I can't leave if I think everything will self-destruct while I'm away. Promise me you won't do anything stupid while I'm gone."

I threw my hands up in the air. "Nothing is going to self-destruct because nothing was going to happen anyway. Levi and I are just friends. That's all we've ever been. Every once in a while, we flirt. It's harmless."

"He knows how I feel about this, Katie. I've always been clear about this with him."

Wait, why would Ollie have had to? Did Levi have feelings for me?

Ollie continued, "Clay brought a prince when Megan said she wanted to meet someone. He might know someone nice for you."

"Ollie?"

"Yes?"

"Shut up."

"Not until you promise me that nothing—"

"Oh, my God. Fine. Even if I want to, I promise I won't fuck Levi," I declared loudly.

Ollie's hand dropped from my shoulder, then a few feet away, Levi said, "You have my key fob, Ollie. I'll meet you two at the truck."

If I could have disappeared into the grass below my feet, I would have. Instead, I glared at Ollie. He opened his mouth to say something, but I raised a finger. "Nope. Don't. Just stop."

A few minutes later, Levi held the passenger door of the truck open for me. It was something Ollie often mocked him for, but Levi had always gone out of his way to make me feel cared for. Not one of us said a word as I scooted over to my spot in the middle.

Ollie climbed in next to me while Levi walked around the truck. Under my breath, I said, "If you value your life, don't say a word. Not one more word."

Ollie slammed the door and sighed.

After opening the driver-side door, Levi met my gaze briefly. The concern in his eyes made me feel better and worse at the same time. He didn't want me to feel uncomfortable and was silently asking if I was okay with him essentially wedging himself against me.

I nodded and looked away.

Ollie, Levi, and I had been riding around in trucks my whole life. As the smallest, I always ended up in the middle. It had never been awkward. But then, Levi had never shown the slightest sign that he might find me attractive. Not sober or drunk. Not when I was engulfed in a winter parka or barely dressed in a bikini. I'd always thought he saw me as nothing more than a little sister.

Was I wrong?

Chapter Four

Levi

"*E*VEN IF *I want to . . .*"
Did she want to?

I've had plenty of bad ideas in my life and I followed through on more than I cared to remember, but she was one I needed to resist. Yes, she was attracted to me. Yes, lately, her heated looks had me imagining doing things with her, to her, that I shouldn't. Knowing that she might be sharing a few of my fantasies was not helping my resolve.

As I drove, I was hyper-aware of every place her body jostled against mine. A man of my experience shouldn't be affected by the innocent way her thigh slid to rest against mine. When I took a turn and her shoulder bumped against me, the warmth from her body was the ultimate tease. She quickly adjusted herself, moving so there was space between us again. I kept both hands on the steering wheel and my gaze straight ahead.

It wasn't as if she'd never touched me before. I wasn't

proud of how many times she'd hauled Ollie and me into the back of someone's truck after we'd partied too hard.

She'd seen me at my best, but she'd also absolutely seen me at my worst. Neither of us spoke about how last year she'd brought me soup because she'd heard I was sick. I'd spiked a high fever and was passed out on my couch in nothing but my underwear. She'd called Ollie's mother and had me downing ibuprofen and in a lukewarm bath before I was fully aware of what was going on.

She liked to joke that she saved my life that day, but she'd also forever changed how I saw her. Until then, she'd been firmly placed in the category of Ollie's cousin—completely off limits even in my thoughts. It didn't matter that the reason she'd stripped me to my underwear was that I'd been nearly delusional. The feel of her hands on my bare skin as well as the tenderness of her touch had haunted my dreams since.

From that day forward, as far as my body was concerned, I could no longer see her as the young girl who'd been my constant shadow. All I could see was the beauty of the woman she'd become.

We pulled up in front of Bradford's house. It was a two-story white farmhouse with a green roofed porch that wrapped around three sides of it. A few months earlier, I would have said that beyond the substantial acreage that came with it, there wasn't much value to the home. However, Bradford and Joanna were renovating it, and as it came back to life, I could see the promise to it.

The barn had been beyond saving, so they'd torn it down and were in the process of building a sprawling one with a large indoor ring as well as housing for their future staff. Joanna already had a mini-horse rescue, but this place would be their primary home, and their second rescue location.

Joanna waved to us from the porch as I parked. Bradford stood beside her. She was a soft-hearted, sweet woman who'd instantly been accepted by the locals. Authentic and kind, that's all we asked of people. Her seemingly happy marriage to Bradford was proof that opposites did attract. I often wondered how much she knew about what he did, but did it matter? With her, his expression softened, and his words were kinder.

She was likely the safest woman on the planet. I couldn't imagine anyone daring to raise as much as an eyebrow at her with Bradford around. They had something special, that was for sure. Good for him, but committing to one person wasn't in my future.

Ollie was the first to break the silence. "You guys mind if I talk to Bradford alone for a minute?"

"No, go ahead," Katie said kindly, surprising me.

"We'll wait here." I regretted those words as soon as I realized it would leave Katie, me, and her earlier declaration in the cab of my truck.

Ollie looked like he was gathering his courage as he opened the passenger door and let himself out. Alone with

Katie, the silence was oppressive.

She watched Ollie go and said, "I don't want to talk about it."

"I don't either." I let out a breath of relief.

"Ollie was—*being Ollie.*"

"I know."

"You know how he drives me crazy sometimes." She clasped her hands on her lap, and it was impossible to look away from her profile. Why did she have to be so damn beautiful? "When I said, 'Even if I want to—'."

"You don't have to explain."

She bit her bottom lip. "I feel like I do. I know you're Ollie's friend, but you're mine too."

My heart started thudding wildly in my chest. "I am."

"I would never want to do anything that would jeopardize that."

My mouth went dry. "Neither would I."

She laughed nervously. "We're not kids anymore and both of us are single, but that doesn't matter because we're practically family."

"Exactly."

"But it would be totally normal to sometimes find each other attractive."

Nope, I wasn't about to touch that one.

She continued, "We're going to be training side by side for a while. I feel like if we don't address this, it might get confusing for one or both of us."

It wasn't confusing to me—it was just a really, *really* bad idea. "We wouldn't want that."

"Right. So, just to be clear, there's nothing for Ollie to worry about."

I cracked the window on my side. "Absolutely nothing."

She blinked a few times quickly. "Good. We're on the same page about this."

"One hundred percent."

"Oh, one more thing." She turned toward me.

I held my breath.

She said, "I know there's more to the computer training than you let on."

I opened my mouth to tell her there wasn't, then she smiled, and my brain emptied.

She gave my thigh a pat and humor filled her eyes. "Did you really think you could lie to someone who knows you as well as I do?"

I laid my hand over hers on my thigh and time stopped. Her mouth parted slightly. A strong desire to taste those sweet lips of hers and pull her fully against me surged as I struggled to remember why I could never act on that feeling. My hand tightened on hers briefly before I moved it off my leg. "I had to try."

There was a flash of hurt in her eyes that gutted me. God, I hated disappointing her. Always had. It wasn't that I didn't want her to touch me. I was grappling with the exact opposite problem.

Whether Ollie was ready for us or not, it was time to get out of the truck. I opened the door, then paused when Katie whispered my name.

Her soft, tentative tone nearly destroyed my resolve. "Even though we'd never do anything about it, I have to know . . . Ollie thinks you're attracted to me . . . are you?"

I gripped the door handle and inhaled sharply without turning to look at her. "I should tell you that I'm not, but I don't want to lie to you twice today."

Chapter Five

Katie

*W*AIT? *What?*

It took me a moment to move from my spot and catch my breath. Yes, I knew he was wrong for me. No, I didn't believe I could be the one to change his womanizing soul, but . . .

Holy four cheese macaroni with bacon bits.

He opened the door for me as he had my entire life, but this time when I slid out to stand beside him, I raised my eyes to meet his and swayed toward him. I tried to remind myself that he'd probably looked down at half the women in Maine exactly the same way he was looking at me, but that didn't stop me from wondering if he was as good at kissing . . . and everything else . . . as women whispered he was.

The air was electric with tension as we stood there just looking into each other's eyes.

From a few feet away, Joanna said, "Could I offer either

of you a water? A snack? You're welcome to come in and freshen up if you'd like. Putting up a fence is hard work."

I meant to answer her.

Levi didn't respond either. His gaze settled on my lips and his nostrils flared.

Joanna chuckled. "Well, we're all inside when you're ready. Just come on in."

Levi's expression hardened and his hands clenched at his sides. "We're not doing this, Katie."

There was no sense pretending I didn't know what he was referring to. "I never said we were."

"So stop looking at me like that."

"You're looking right back at me the same way."

His lips pressed together in a tight line then he muttered, "I don't do relationships. I have sex with women who understand that and don't see me as a challenge."

I frowned at that. "I don't see you as a challenge."

"No? So you're just looking for fun with no expectations?"

"No."

"How many men have you been with, Katie?"

My chin rose. He knew, he just wanted to drive a point home. "One," I muttered.

"The douche you left town with?"

My temper lit. "I'm not doing this. I made a mistake but that was years ago. Let it go."

He frowned. "Do you know where he is now? Prison.

You'd think the beating he received from Cooper and your brother would have set him straight, but people don't change."

I looked away, not wanting to think about that day. Levi cupped my chin with one hand and raised my face until my eyes met his again. "People don't change," he said firmly. "Not him. Not me."

"Don't compare yourself to him. You'd never hurt a woman."

His hand dropped and his shoulders rolled back. "Not physically, but before I learned to be brutally honest, I broke a few hearts. I'm not proud of that. At the end of the day, I never care enough to stay." He tapped his chest. "People say I should feel something when I walk away but—nothing. No matter how good the sex is."

My heart broke a little for him then even as I hugged my arms protectively around myself. "At least the sex is good." My joke fell flat.

"That would never be enough for you."

"You're right. Then Ollie would break your neck."

A slight smile pulled at his lips. "He'd try."

I swallowed hard. "Ollie said I'm the only thing he can imagine your friendship ending over. That's what he was saying to me. He wanted me to promise I wouldn't do anything stupid because if it ended badly, and he believed it would, everything would fall apart. People would take sides. Ultimately, you'd be the one who was hurt more."

"Then it's a good thing we're too smart to act on something that is nothing more than a fleeting attraction."

I nodded. "Fleeting."

We stood there, so close, yet so far from each other. He cleared his throat. "We'll get through this, Katie. And someday you'll end up with a wonderful man who'll rock your world and stay. And I'll be right there at your wedding, celebrating your choice, because we *are* like family."

The pain in his eyes was more than I could take. I wrapped my arms around him and buried my face in his strong chest. It was an impulsive decision I would have said I made out of sympathy for him, but there was no denying the fire that shot through me as his hands settled on my hips. Against his shirt, I mumbled, "I hate you a little bit right now."

His chest rumbled with a laugh. "I'm hating my over-eager cock, so you should probably stop rubbing yourself against it."

"I am not—" His excitement was indeed growing in size against me. Blushing, I stepped back. "Sorry."

He shook his head as if to clear it and gave me the lop-sided smile he reserved for close friends. "Don't be. I'm not complaining. But, like you said, it's better if neither of us gets confused."

I had said that. And I'd meant it. So what the hell was I doing?

"Bradford would like to see you guys," Ollie called unhappily from the porch.

A quick glance at his face confirmed he'd seen too much. I sighed. "I'll talk to him."

"No," Levi said. "You don't have to explain yourself to him. Nor do I." He bent closer until his lips hovered over mine and growled, "If I thought I'd be any good for you, nothing Ollie could say or do would keep me from you."

A shiver of desire shot through me. Levi always had been one to live by his own rules. Did every woman feel this wanton and beautiful when he looked at her that way? Knowing the attraction was mutual overshadowed my common sense. Had we been alone, I doubt our clothing would have stayed on.

"We should go," I said in a strangled voice.

He nodded and stepped back.

Only once there was distance between us did my breathing return to normal.

Side by side we made our way to where Ollie was standing on the porch. Although it looked like there was a lot more he wanted to say, he muttered, "I'm leaving tonight for Boston. It's too good of an opportunity to refuse."

"I'm glad," Levi responded.

I could have told Ollie I was aware that something else was going on, but it was obviously important to him that no one knew so I forced a bright smile. "Don't forget your promise to teach me everything you learn when you get back."

"I won't," Ollie said quietly. "It'll also be good for me to get away and clear my head. When I come back, Katie, I'll be a whole lot nicer than I've been lately."

I rushed forward and hugged him. "Don't make empty promises; you've never been nice."

His arms tightened around me as he chuckled. "Ah, my sweet, sweet cousin. I'll miss you."

I stepped back, this time with a genuine smile. "I'll miss you, too."

"Do you need extra help at Little Willie's while you're gone?" Levi asked. "Especially since Katie will be otherwise occupied."

The look Ollie gave Levi was comically dark. "With?"

Levi spread his hands wide in the air. "Putting up fences? Working out? Learning self-defense moves? With both of you gone, who'll work the restaurant?"

Ollie seemed to relax a little. "My mother was stepping in while we did this training. That won't change. Everette said he doesn't mind covering some shifts."

"I can help out as well . . . around whatever Bradford has us doing," Levi said.

"I'll pick up extra shifts too," I offered.

Ollie's stance softened. "I'd appreciate that. I don't want Mom doing too much and it would be good to have some-one looking in on her. Worst case, we close early a few days."

I gushed, "We'll keep everything going while you're gone. Don't worry."

"I know." His shoulders rose and fell. "Mind if I take the truck, Levi? I'll come back later to pick you guys up. If I'm actually leaving tonight, I'll need to pack . . . and tell Mom. That part won't be easy."

"Just be honest," I said. "She'll be happy for you."

Ollie pinned Levi with a look. "Honest about what?"

Crap. "About there only being one slot and how we all thought you were the best suited for it." Then in a light tone, I added, "Expect her to ask why I didn't get it. You know she loves me more."

Ollie rolled his eyes and looked relieved. "Don't steal my room while I'm gone."

I laughed. "What a great idea. Oh, wait, it smells like old socks. I'll pass. Besides, why would I want to give up the drafty splendor of my room above my parents' garage?"

"If the drive gets to be too much, Katie, you can always stay at my place," Levi said with a smirk.

My mouth dropped open, and heat flooded my face, until I realized that Levi was joking. Of course he was joking. I lived one town over. There wasn't a need for me to stay overnight in Driverton.

Yet.

I gave myself a stern mental shake. *Stop.*

Ollie cursed and shook his head. "You shouldn't mess with me like that."

Levi grinned. "If I didn't, would we even be best friends?"

Shaking his head while he smiled, Ollie said, "Payback will happen. Not sure when or how, but count on it."

Levi tossed him his key fob. Ollie caught it midair. "Call me if you need anything, Katie. I can be home in a few hours, and if you have any questions about Little Willie's or anything don't worry about what time it is—"

I laid a hand on his arm. "Go. Everything will be here and fine when you get back."

After shooting Levi one last look, Ollie left.

As I watched him drive away, I said, "Levi, thank you for whatever you set up for Ollie. You're a good friend."

He made a sound deep in his throat before answering. "He would have done it for me." His smile was sad. "You would have too."

"That's very true." A heaviness settled over my chest. I loved Levi. I wasn't in love with him, but he had a special place in my heart. I knew why he didn't care when he walked away from the women he chose to be with. I even understood why he sought out women he'd never have to see again. He'd told me once when he was drunk. It wasn't because he was a horrible person or that he couldn't feel anything. It was deeper and sadder than that. I didn't bring up that conversation, because the secrets friends share when they're inebriated are not supposed to be remembered. Unfortunately for him, I was often the person serving the alcohol rather than drinking it. My memories weren't muddled.

Until recently, and this stupid attraction I felt for Levi, my feelings weren't either. None of us were perfect. I'd nearly given up on doing more than working for Ollie and getting by until Bradford found Cooper and we were all given incredible opportunities.

Cooper was now happily married and proudly making a difference in so many lives.

Everette was as well.

Their lives were filled with not just love, but purpose. I wanted that—and the confidence that came with challenging myself to do better.

"Levi?"

"Yes."

"I *do* think I can run faster than you can."

He coughed on a laugh, then a louder one rumbled out of him. "You're on."

Chapter Six

Levi

KATIE AND I went inside and headed into different bathrooms to freshen up and wash off the layers of dirt we'd brought with us from the field. I was walking through the house in search of Bradford when I heard him talking to his wife and, not wanting to intrude, stopped before entering the room.

"What do you think you're doing?" His tone was surprisingly harsh. I'd never seen him so much as frown at Joanna.

She didn't appear bothered by it when she answered cheerfully, "Since you were planning to train three people anyway and now there are only two, I thought it'd be the perfect time for you to put me through your boot camp. I'd love to tone up."

"You're beautiful the way you are."

"Thank you," she said with a laugh. "But I want to do this. It wouldn't be a bad idea for me to learn self-defense and how to shoot a gun. I think it would be fun."

"No," he snapped.

Ouch. I told myself to walk away. None of this was any of my business, but I held Bradford in near hero status in my mind. All that would change if where this went even hinted that he wasn't kind to Joanna.

I'd never seen her with bruises, but I'd seen more than a few on my mother before my father left the first time. If Bradford laid a hand on Joanna, the fury I'd unleash would trump his Special Forces training. So, I stood there, tense, and ready.

"I'm doing it," she said.

"You are not."

"I am. I'll need the skills if I'm going to be part of what you're building here in Driverton. Clay said I could work with—"

"No. I won't allow it."

"Allow it?" Her voice lowered and I sucked in a breath. He wasn't about to hurt her, but he was treading on dangerous territory. What was he thinking? "Did you think I could live in a town where everyone is learning how to rescue lost children and not want to be a part of that?"

"That's the problem? Solved. We leave."

"Bradford—"

"This isn't something I'm willing to budge on. Pack up your stuff. I'll make a few calls. We'll ship the minis to our other farm."

"No. I want to be a part of what's going on here."

"Not going to happen."

"Will you at least hear me out?"

"I'll give you a choice. We stay and you drop this, or we leave."

"Really? How about this for a choice? You can finish this conversation by yourself or . . . oh, yes, you can finish it by yourself because I won't be spoken to like I'm a child."

"Joanna—"

She rushed past me so quickly I wasn't sure she'd seen me. I heard Bradford swear from the next room. Some might have taken that as a cue to leave, but Bradford was my friend. I stepped inside and didn't flinch when the look he shot me was far from friendly.

I pocketed my hands and shrugged. "So, I couldn't help but overhear—"

"Take Katie and go home. I won't be training anyone."

Clearing my throat, I didn't move an inch. "If you want to talk . . ."

"You heard me," he barked. "Go."

I sighed and sat in the overstuffed chair nearest to me. Joanna had definitely chosen it. Nothing about Bradford was warm or cozy. "Sit down."

The look he gave me was one that would have probably had someone who didn't know him shaking in their shoes. Regardless of what Bradford did on his missions, he was a good person, and his beef wasn't with me.

So I repeated myself. "Sit."

Fists clenched, he paced in front of me. "This isn't happening."

"What isn't happening?"

"Joanna can't work with us."

"Why?"

He stopped and glared down at me. When he spoke, his voice was raw. "She's everything to me."

Yeah. I got that. "You should probably lead with that when you apologize to her."

"I'm not sorry. I won't put her in danger. Never. Nothing she could say would convince me."

"It's okay to be afraid, Bradford. It's not okay to lay the weight of your fear on someone else."

"I'm not—" He stopped, then rubbed a hand across his eyes. "I can't lose her too."

"I know."

"I'd give up everything for her—my very soul if she needed it."

"She could train with you then work on a safe part of the jobs we get. Everette decided he didn't enjoy dodging bullets. There are ways she could help without putting her in danger."

He was quiet for several long minutes before he said, "I live two very different lives. One is full of love, kindness, mini horses, and Joanna. The other . . ."

"Yeah." I stood. "The thing is, Bradford, I don't think Joanna wants to live in only one of your lives. I'm not suggesting you take her on the missions, but if she's asking to be a part of your team here—doesn't she deserve a chance to be?"

"You don't understand. I've done things . . ."

"That you don't want her to see."

"Exactly."

"So this is about more than protecting her. It's about protecting you."

He frowned. "It's about both, I guess."

"That's also what she needs to hear."

He shook his head. "What am I supposed to say? Joanna, I love you so much I'm terrified of losing you? Too much to risk letting you see what I really do?"

"Yes," from the doorway, Joanna answered in a gentle voice. "I know what you do, Bradford, and the price you pay to do what others can't or won't. There's no risk to letting me in. I love you."

His lips pressed together, and he blinked a few times quickly.

She rushed forward, right into his arms. "When you leave to find someone, I can't sleep right. I'm just as afraid of losing you as you are of losing me."

He buried his face in her hair as I began to back out of the room.

She continued, "I don't want to be on the outside looking in. I don't have to go with you on the jobs, but I want to help you bring those kids home. Let me be part of it."

Whatever he answered was lost to me as I rounded the corner and came face to face with Katie in the hallway. Our eyes met and I didn't have to ask her how much she'd heard. Her voice was just above a whisper. "For someone who doesn't do relationships, you're good at helping others navigate them."

I shrugged the compliment off. "No one wants to see someone they love put themselves in danger."

She nodded slowly then looked past me to where Bradford and Joanna were talking. "Do you think Bradford will still want to train us?"

"I don't know."

Turning her attention back to me, she asked, "I feel weird standing here waiting for them to work this out. We could call Ollie to come pick us up."

"It's only a few miles to his house. We could walk back."

"Or run." Her expression was pure innocence.

A chuckle burst from me. "You're itching to show me that you're faster than I am, aren't you?"

A smile pulled at her lips. "Maybe."

"Fine. You're on."

As we made our way to the door, she asked, "Should we wager something? First one to Ollie's house wins."

I tripped over nothing but quickly righted myself. "What do you have in mind?" My traitorous thoughts were filling with several options and none of them were a good idea. If Bradford did cancel our training, I was beginning to think it would be for the best. Things were changing between Katie and me, and it was probably better to spend some time away from each other to cool the situation down.

We were in the driveway before she answered. "Since I'm definitely going to win, it should be something you wouldn't normally agree to."

Oh, man, the front of my jeans tightened as, against my will, my excitement surged. "Your confidence is adorable, but what if I counter with something equally normally off the table for you?" I dipped my head toward her and smiled. "And win."

She ran the tip of her tongue across her bottom lip. "You think I'm afraid of a challenge?"

God, I shouldn't want her, but I do. "You should be."

"If I win"—She placed a hand flat on my chest and my heart started beating so wildly I was certain she could feel it—"you have to . . ."

Anything. In that moment, I would have thrown all caution and loyalty to the wind and agreed to whatever she wanted. "Yes?"

"Work all of my morning shifts while Ollie is away."

Disappointment. Desire. Frustration. It all tumbled through me. I should have been relieved, but her hand remained on my chest, jumbling my thoughts. I couldn't share the list of things I was compiling. A kiss. A night in her bed. A taste of her sex before I fed her my cock. Nope. We'd agreed to avoid all that. In a strangled voice, I said, "Then if

I win, you will clean out my basement."

Getting rid of everything associated with my parents was something I'd considered doing for a long time, but Bradford's question about them had brought it to the forefront of my thoughts. Would I want to ever look for them? Hell no. Was it time to shed all of their shit? Absolutely. Well past when I should have.

Her hand pushed on my chest. "That creepy, damp dungeon that looks like it's prepping for an episode of *Hoarders*?"

"You're the one who set the rules. We don't have to race. We could always walk like two perfectly normal people."

Her hand dropped and she bent to a sprint position. "See you at Ollie's." Without waiting for me, she took off at an impressively fast pace. Never having been a runner, I chose a slower, steady beat that I hoped would allow me to at least not collapse halfway to Ollie's. Katie disappeared around the corner of the road. *Looks like I'll be getting up early on the daily until Ollie gets back.*

I didn't really mind. Little Willie's wasn't your average restaurant. Very rarely was there a customer who wasn't from Driverton. If asked, the regulars would not only clear off their own tables, but when Ollie was in a financial bind, meals there became more of a potluck. Ollie's family was known for being generous with the community and because of that, the people of Driverton were generous with him. I supplied his restaurant with free produce on a regular basis because the Williams were one of the reasons I never ended up in foster care or jail. They were one of the families who stepped in when my parents left. They made sure I finished high school and that the bills on my small farm continued to be paid until I could take over and pay them myself. That's the kind of debt you can never fully repay, but I did my best to on the daily.

Nowhere was perfect. Driverton had a reputation for being a little rough. Neighboring towns tended to consider it a place that was best to drive around. That was mostly due to a few run-ins we'd had with people who'd dropped by to fuck around and found out that we had no problem handling things on our own. In fact, we preferred it that way. The only reason we tolerated a sheriff was because Tom was Katie's older brother and Ollie's cousin. Like Katie, Tom had spent enough of his childhood running around Driverton that he could never be considered an outsider.

I took a shortcut through the woods. Was it cheating? I didn't think so. We hadn't agreed to any particular route to Ollie's, and I didn't care if I won. Ollie's house had seemed a lot closer before I'd started running. Katie was right, I hadn't run anywhere since . . . ever? Out of breath and sweating, I came across Katie sitting on a log on the side of the walking path.

I stopped abruptly next to her, bent over, breathing heavily. "Taking a break?"

She waved at her ankle. "I twisted it. I can walk on it, but it hurts, so I'm taking a break before I keep going."

"Let me see it." My discomfort disappeared in the face of

hers. She raised her leg, and I clasped a hand around her calf. Her ankle was a little swollen. "You should have called me."

She pursed her lips before saying, "I was hoping I could still win."

Still holding her leg, I arched an eyebrow. "Hold on, you're sitting down and when you get up, you'll probably be hobbling. How did you think you could still beat me?"

She looked away. "I didn't know you knew about this shortcut." When her gaze returned to meet mine, she said, "We never said we had to stay on the road. And clearly you're okay with it since you're here."

That brought a smile to my face. "I'm not judging. I'm impressed." Her face flushed and I realized I'd been absently stroking the side of her calf. I stopped, put her leg down gently, and cleared my throat. "Do you want me to carry you?"

"You can do that?" she asked so seriously my ego cringed.

"*Can* I carry you?" I had to think about it. She wasn't tiny. "I'm a hundred percent sure I could lift you, seventy-five percent sure I could haul you to at least the road."

The look she gave me held irritation at first, then amusement. "You're an asshole."

"It won't be easy, but I'll give it my best shot." Really, I was just giving her shit. It was what we did.

"If Bradford does take us on, I'm going to tell him you need to work on your upper body strength."

Oh, yeah? "*Really*, then I'll tell him . . ." I looked her

over from head to toe and back. Her face was devoid of makeup and shining from the run. She was rounded in all the places a woman should be. Great ass. Great everything. Too damn beautiful to make any of this easy. "There's not a thing I'd change about you."

Her mouth rounded then snapped shut.

I'd said the last part out loud and for a moment neither of us knew what to do about that.

Chapter Seven

Katie

I COULD WALK to the road. I'd done double shifts at Little Willie's on worse, but like a moth drawn to a flame I craved his touch again. Looking down at my ankle, I flexed it and deliberately winced. "I'll be fine."

I should have felt guilty when his concern was immediate. "Don't. I was only joking. I could easily carry you all the way to Ollie's. Stand up."

Accepting the hand he held out to help me up, there was a flutter of excitement but not a shred of guilt. "You don't have to—"

Whoosh, he swept me off my feet and across his chest. I steadied myself by putting an arm over his muscled shoulder, my hand cupping the back of his neck. There was nothing weak about him and I marveled at how long it had taken me to realize how strong he was. My body warmed in anticipation of what we'd both said wouldn't happen. *So this is what it's like to want someone. Crave to be taken by them.* It made what I'd felt for other men seem like childish crushes. He inhaled sharply as if he could read my thoughts.

"You okay?" he asked in a husky voice that only had me melting against him more.

I took a moment to answer, hoping I wouldn't give anything away when I did. "Yeah."

Without another word he began to walk toward the road. I rested my head on his shoulder, closed my eyes, and allowed myself to savor the moment. If any other man had offered to carry me, I would have seen it as a romantic gesture. Levi would be the first one to tell you he didn't have a romantic bone in his body. Still, that didn't stop me from feeling protected and treasured.

"This is exactly what we shouldn't be doing," Levi said gruffly.

Sure we were playing with fire, but now that I knew we were both fighting the same urges the awkwardness was gone. Friends didn't let friends say stupid shit without calling them out. I chuckled against his chest. "If I'm too much of a temptation, you can put me down."

He shifted, adjusting me higher, his arms tightening deliciously around me. "The problem is—I don't want to."

My eyes flew open. Had he just said what I thought he did? There was so much I wanted to say . . . to ask, but I didn't want to ruin the moment.

He continued, "And, just to clarify, being carried back to the road is a clear disqualifier. I won the race."

That had my eyes opening and my head whipping back. "You little cheater. I'm not cleaning your basement. I demand a do-over."

With that smooth grin of his, he glanced down at me. "You're a sore loser. I'll help you drive everything to the dump."

"The dump?"

"It's time for it to go."

Someone who didn't know him well wouldn't have understood how sad that was. Throughout high school, he'd left the house exactly as his parents had—as if expecting them to return. The day after graduation, he'd boxed everything that had belonged to his parents and put it in his basement. "Have you—did something happen?"

"No."

When we reached the end of the path, he slowly lowered me to my feet, but kept an arm around my waist to steady me. "I'll call Ollie," he said.

I glanced around and spotted Levi's truck coming down the road. "Looks like you don't have to."

Ollie pulled over to the side of the road and got out. Pinning Levi with an angry look, Ollie said, "Joanna called and said you two might need a ride."

Not moving from my side, Levi answered easily, "We didn't think we did, but Katie twisted her ankle."

For a second Ollie didn't look like he believed Levi, but when he saw how I was standing on only one leg, he seemed to relax. "How bad?"

I shook my head dismissively. "I just rolled it. If I wrap it tonight I'm sure it'll be fine by tomorrow."

"Good thing Levi was there."

"Yeah," I said. The details didn't matter.

"Can you make it to the truck?" Ollie asked.

I glanced up at Levi whose face was as carefully blank as mine. "If Levi doesn't mind helping me over there."

"I don't mind," Levi said curtly.

Slowly, with Levi's arm around my waist, I hobbled over to his truck. This time it was Ollie who opened the passenger door. I climbed in and slid over to my usual spot, Ollie and Levi stood there for a moment, doing something only best friends can, having a whole conversation without uttering a word. Eventually Ollie handed Levi his key fob and climbed into the truck next to me.

I glanced at Levi when he joined us but there was no hint of what he was thinking. When he started up the truck, I asked Ollie, "Did you tell your mother yet that you're going away?"

He nodded. "She doesn't love the idea of any of us working with Bradford, but she thinks a few computer courses could be good for me."

That didn't sound right to me. "I thought she liked him."

Ollie turned to look out the window as Levi pulled back onto the road. "She likes *him*. She's just afraid that one of us will get hurt. Can't blame her after what almost happened to Everette."

"That's understandable." Everette's attempt to help find a missing woman had landed him tied up next to her in the freezer of two serial killers. If Shelby hadn't convinced us to go looking for him, both he and the woman he'd sought would have been two more of their victims.

"I should probably drop Katie off first. We don't want your mother thinking we broke her on the first day," Levi said.

I let out a sad sigh. "Unless Bradford changes his mind it might also be our last day."

"What did I miss?" Ollie asked.

We told him because there were no secrets between us. Well, at least, there never had been. Plus, the outcome of Bradford's talk with Joanna would affect all three of us.

"Holy shit," Ollie said. "Joanna didn't seem upset so they must have talked it out."

"I hope so," Levi said quietly.

I studied a blister that had formed on the palm of one of my hands. "Do you know how many times I've given up on something because I doubted myself? It's why I never went to college and have pretty much given up on men. I don't know when we stopped believing good things could happen for us, but I'm done living like that. We all agreed to pick each other up if we fell, but we need to promise each other more than that. No matter what happens with Bradford—we keep going. We don't need someone else to believe in us as long as we believe in each other. We can do this."

Ollie and Levi nodded and that was as good as a handshake to me.

A few minutes later, Levi parked his truck in my parents' driveway. When Ollie hopped out, Levi said, "I'll text you if I hear from Bradford."

I laughed. "I'll be working the breakfast shift. You know, the one I wouldn't have to if I hadn't twisted my ankle. The one I'll have to suffer through, hour after hour, probably in agony . . ."

Ollie looked back and forth between us then frowned "I can put off going to Boston for another day."

Across the cab, Levi said, "No, I'll work it. Rest your ankle, Katie."

"You just want me to heal so I don't renege on our deal."

Ollie didn't sound all that pleased with that option. "What kind of 'deal' do you and Katie have?"

Rather than answering him, I gave Ollie a hug. "Stop worrying. If you want, I can call you every day while you're away."

His arms closed around me even as he said, "So mean—threatening me like that."

Laughing, I stepped back. "Twice a day if you're not careful."

He raised his hands in surrender. "Okay. Okay. I get it. I'm worrying over nothing."

Levi and I exchanged a quick, guilty glance, then looked away. Ollie wasn't imagining something that wasn't there. Something had changed between Levi and me that day. Now my breath caught each time he looked at me. Could we go back to how we were before? Did I want to? I didn't know.

Levi had earned his bad reputation with women, but was that how he'd be with me? We weren't strangers, weren't an out-of-town hookup.

We were—

I didn't know what we were anymore and that was scary and more than a little exciting. As Ollie got back into the truck, I looked past him and said, "Levi, I'll come in and set up for lunch. Aunt Reana will be there so even if I can't do too much, I can help her find everything."

"Sounds good," was all he said.

Ollie closed the door and waved before they drove off. I was making my way to the stairway on the side of my parents' detached garage when I heard the crunch of gravel behind me. For a second, I thought it might be Levi and Ollie returning, but it was my parents. My mother waved me over.

My father was a seasoned firefighter; serious and reserved but loving. Although there was gray peppering his hair now, he still had a presence most people instantly decided not to mess with. If there was something he was afraid of, I wasn't aware of it. My mother worked as a nurse in the emergency room of a city hospital over an hour away. She was soft and sweet on the outside with a whole lot of steel and fire beneath that.

They'd met in high school, dated, and never separated. My mother joked that she didn't have a choice in the matter. She said when you meet a man who'll walk without complaint through hell for you and take your side in any fight without needing to determine if you're right, he's a keeper.

My father's devotion to my mother was clear in how he hadn't tried to change her mind when she said she wanted to move to wherever her brother, Ollie's father, did. We didn't talk much about my mother's side of the family, but I knew they'd never approved of Aunt Reana and that was enough for me not to like them.

Ollie's parents had been young and in search of a more accepting place when their car had broken down in Driverton and they stayed. I once asked my mother why she and Dad had chosen a house in a neighboring town. She said it was because they hadn't found a house in Driverton. I suspected they'd wanted more than Driverton could offer. They also both had jobs that required a larger population. The town they'd chosen had several restaurants . . . as well as its own police station and even a movie theater. It was still small enough that my brother handled more domestic disputes than actual crimes and most people knew each other, but it wasn't nearly as close-knit as Driverton was.

My parents were okay with that last part. They liked their privacy. Tom was the same. Me? I loved Driverton. I'd even had my own room at Aunt Reana's house until I was old enough to drive.

Both of my parents were out of the car before I reached it. My mother looked me over then waved at my injured ankle. "Hurt on your first day? I told you it wasn't a good idea."

"I'm fine, Mom. I tripped and twisted it. That's all."

My father stepped closer to inspect. "Doesn't look so bad. We'll ice and wrap it. I'd take it easy tomorrow."

"I will. Levi's covering my morning shift."

A mother's intuition is nothing to underestimate. "Levi? Why not Ollie?"

"Bradford is sending Ollie out of town for a computer course."

One of her eyebrows arched. "That's the first I'm hearing of this."

I shrugged. "Just found out about it today, but it was too good of an opportunity for Ollie to not jump on."

"There wasn't room for you in that course?" Had my mother not gone into nursing, she would have made an effective interrogator. Visible crumbs had never been necessary for her to know when I'd snuck a cookie.

"Not this time, no. But that's okay because I'm excited about starting the training the way Everette did."

"I don't remember Everette getting hurt on his first day."

"Mom." Everything I couldn't say poured out in the way I said her name as a plea.

My father grunted, then said, "You can't expect us to not worry."

"I know how lucky I am to have parents who care." I looked back and forth between the two of them. "But you guys were married and had Tom by my age. This is my chance to do something with my life."

"Sorry if I don't want my little girl getting killed trying to prove something to all these rich people Cooper brought to Driverton. Don't pin your hopes on them. They're nothing like us and Driverton is just a temporary playground to people like that."

"You don't know them, Mom. And the only one I'm trying to prove something to is myself."

My mother set her head at a stubborn angle I knew too well from childhood. "There's not one part of this I approve of."

Despite the wordless plea I sent my father, he remained silent. I said, "It doesn't require your approval." When I saw in her eyes that she felt it did, I added, "You've always said this is your house and therefore your rules, and if you want me to move out I will, but . . ."

"No one is asking you to move out," my father said quietly.

My mother's expression remained set in stone. "Don't try emotional blackmail on me, young lady. You're old enough that *running away* is not a threat."

My temper began to rise. "All I'm trying to say is that

I'm an adult and should be able to live my life on my terms."

"Above our garage for free?" my mother volleyed, and I sucked in an audible breath.

"Rose," my father said my mother's name in a low tone. "This isn't what you want." He directed his next comment to me. "It's not what any of us want."

He was right. I rarely argued with my mother. She wasn't trying to tear my confidence down or get me to move out. I doubted it was even about the money. All she wanted was for me to find my way and soar. Still, criticism from her cut deep. "I've offered to pay rent for the space."

"You barely make enough at Little Willie's to afford your car and phone." She sighed. "The last thing I want is for you to waitress more to pay us. You should consider going back to school instead of chasing this wild dream of being some kind of private detective. What you need to be doing is thinking about the next step in your life. What do you want? Where do you want to be in five . . . ten years from now? And what are you doing to get yourself there?"

It was not a fun conversation to have, but it was one we'd danced around many times in the prior weeks. To finally face it head-on was somewhat of a relief. An unexpected bonus of being put in a place where I needed to defend my decisions was that it helped clarify to myself what I wanted. "I love working in Driverton, Mom. Where would I like to see myself in five or ten years? Right there, in a house I found a way to pay for. I know you have trouble understanding why, but even when I secure a second and better source of income, and I will, I intend to continue working at Little Willie's. It is more than just a restaurant or bar. It's the community-funded heart of the town. Working there and helping people brings me a lot of satisfaction."

"This isn't about Driverton, it's about the kind of people you're beginning to associate with."

As my head began to pound, I pressed two fingers to my temple and circled the area. "Money doesn't make someone evil, Mom. Just like the lack of it doesn't lower someone's morals. These are good people. If you don't want to take the time to get to know them, you'll just have to trust my judgment."

"Your brother agrees with me that what you're doing isn't safe. Not only does he not want you working with Bradford, but he also told me how close you came to getting yourself killed when you involved yourself in Everette's last *mission*."

There it was—the real issue my mother had with me training with Bradford. She blamed him as well as Cooper's family for a situation they'd played no role in creating. "You're right, it was dangerous, but Ollie, Levi, Shelby and I saved two lives that day. What would you have had me do? Nothing? Everette would be dead and so would that woman." Striving to keep my tone kind and respectful, I added, "When Dad goes into a burning house to save someone, there's a chance he won't come out—but he wouldn't be the man you love if he was okay with playing it safe and watching someone die."

My father tucked my mother against his side in quiet support. She clasped her hands in front of her, lips still pressed together in a stern line.

I continued, "Your work involves danger as well. You deal with new diseases, people on drugs, and everything in between. And you've told me you like the emergency room better than quieter parts of the hospital because it's where you feel you make the biggest impact. And Tom? You can't tell me his job isn't dangerous. So, unless all of you are ready to retire to the safety of desk jobs, could you please take responsibility for raising me to believe I should also make a difference and accept my choice of how I'll do that."

For a long moment we stood in silent standoff, then my mother said, "God, you take after your father."

My father seemed to be holding back a smile. "Really? I was about to say she sounds like you." When my mother shot him a look, he smiled and added, "In the best way."

When my mother's gaze met mine again, she said, "I love you and respect that you need this, so I'll go along with it, but only because your points made too much damn sense for me to argue, and I want you to be happy."

"Welcome to my world," my father murmured. "That's what I've been saying for nearly forty years."

The look my parents exchanged was so full of love my chest tightened with emotion. Would I ever be loved that way, or was what they had the equivalent of winning the lottery? Rare. A beautiful thing to dream about, but unrealistic to hope for?

What did I want my life to be like in five years? Ten? I wanted everything I'd listed, but also to have someone to share it with. And children. No childhood was perfect, but mine had been such a happy one that I wanted to raise a family and give them the kind of happy home I'd had. It wasn't marriage that I craved, but the solid partnership my parents had.

Against my better judgment, I allowed my thoughts to drift to Levi. He was patient and kind. I could imagine children trotting after him, asking endless questions he'd never tire of answering. If he ever did settle down, he'd make a wonderful father. How would he be as a husband? Could he be faithful to one woman? I wasn't sure if even he knew the answer to that question.

"If Ollie is leaving town, does that mean Reana will be working his shifts?" my mother asked, bringing my thoughts back to the present.

"Some. Levi and I are also helping out more."

"I'll call her and see what we can do. I'm home early most days."

My father added, "And I have a few days off. When is Ollie coming back?"

"A few weeks?" I was glad they were taking the story of where Ollie was going at face value.

Nodding in approval, my mother said, "Ollie's always loved technology. I hope this brings new opportunities to him."

"He'll be doing what I'll be doing, Mom, while still running Little Willie's. Nothing will really change."

My parents exchanged another look that neither of them shared the meaning of. Instead, my mother invited me to eat dinner in the main house. Did I want roast beef club sandwiches with bacon, lettuce, tomatoes, and everything? *Um, yes!*

"We'll look at that ankle at the same time," my father said.

I gingerly put my weight on my injured leg as I took a step toward them. I winced, but it wasn't nearly as bad as it had been when it had first happened. "I'd love that."

Rushing over, my mother took one of my arms by the elbow. "Here, let me be your crutch until we get you inside to a chair."

"It's not that bad, Mom." I took another step which was much more comfortable due to her absorbing the impact of it. "But thank you."

With love in her eyes, she said, "I don't always agree with you, but I'll always be here for you."

God, that sounded like something Levi would say. I held back a smile. She wouldn't appreciate the comparison. Like Driverton, Levi had qualities my mother had difficulty seeing.

If I ever wanted to stop her from focusing on me working with Bradford, all I'd have to do was mention that I was attracted to Levi. Oh, yes, she'd have a lot to say about that and not much good. My father wouldn't voice his opinion, but he'd give me the same look he gave me the day I told him I'd decided against going to college. Although they didn't know Levi as well as I did, they were well acquainted with his reputation.

As I made my way into the house with my parents, my thoughts filled with the memory of being carried by Levi. Beneath his big talk and bad choices, there was a good man who didn't deserve the hand life had dealt him—a man who'd said he would be right there at my wedding, celebrating my decision to be with someone else.

I tried and failed to imagine being happy to see him promise his loyalty and future to another woman. My feelings on that subject must have shown on my face, because my father asked, "Are you in more pain than you're admitting?"

Oddly, stupidly, I was—but the ache I felt wasn't in my ankle.

Chapter Eight

Levi

E ARLY AFTERNOON, I carried another box of what I guessed was clothing to the bottom of the stairs and laid it there. I'd wondered if emptying the basement would make me sad, but I felt nothing. The boy who'd mourned his parents and, alone in this house, had cried himself to sleep more than he cared to remember was long gone and with him whatever feelings I'd had for the people who hadn't considered me important enough to stick around for.

Katie, her ankle wrapped in an ACE bandage, was seated on an old lawn chair. No makeup, hair tied back in a messy ponytail, clad in jeans and a simple flowered sleeveless blouse, Katie was painfully, distractingly beautiful.

I should have called off the bet.

The less time we spent together, the better. At least until we both came back to our senses. I'd never lusted after Katie. As far as I knew, she'd never felt that way about me until recently. It was logical, therefore, to believe that ours was a situation that would rectify itself as long as we were careful.

And careful was what I'd decided to be until she'd shown up at Little Willie's and asked if I'd heard from Bradford. I'd hated admitting that I hadn't. When her expression crumpled and she turned those big sad eyes on me, every shred of sense flew right out of my head. In its place was the undeniable need to protect her from disappointment and an inability to say no to her.

When she'd asked if I wanted to start on my basement that day, I told her she should rest instead. She said she needed to stay busy because she was quietly going crazy wondering what Bradford would decide. Was our second chance with him over before it had begun?

"If you bring me a box, I'll help you sort through it," she said.

"No need. It's all going to the dump."

She stood and gingerly made her way to the side of the basement I was pulling boxes from. "You can't take all this to the dump. Clothing could be rehomed to people who could use it. I see dishes over there. Is that a photo album? Or a scrapbook?"

Instead of answering her question, I said, "You're welcome to take anything you want, but none of this is staying and I don't care where it ends up." Her attention, though, remained on the one item I wish I'd found first and stashed somewhere.

"Seriously, it looks familiar." It was impossible to look

away as she stretched on her tiptoes to reach for the album. The hem of her shirt rose along with her arm, revealing a delicious expanse of skin. The shelf was tall enough to frustrate Katie. She hopped on her good leg in an attempt to reach the corner of the album that protruded from the shelf's edge.

"Stop before you topple the whole thing over."

"Then get it down for me . . . please."

If I hadn't known what it was, I might have. "No."

She whipped around to face me. *"No?"*

"This was a bad idea. Are you okay to drive home on your own?"

"I drove here . . . so, yes. But—"

"Good, then I'll walk you to your car."

She turned and steadied herself by holding on to the shelf. "Because you don't want me to see whatever that is? What is it?"

"Something I'm not going to throw away but is none of your business."

She glanced up at the corner of it. "You just made it a thousand times more tempting."

"It sucks to want what you can't have, doesn't it?" The words had rolled off my tongue as a joke, but neither of us laughed. Our eyes met, the temperature in the room sky-rocketed, then we both quickly looked away.

"Can I ask you a question?"

I should have said no. "Sure."

"If this thing that Cooper and Bradford are doing falls through. Let's say none of it actually happens. What will you do?"

"Do?"

"Will you look for something else like it? Do you have a backup plan?"

"Besides sobriety, no."

"My parents don't think we should be working with Bradford at all. They think it's too dangerous."

"They're often right."

Her gaze flew to meet mine again. "Wow. What happened to the motivational speeches? You said you're all in "

"I am."

"Then why do you sound like you don't care if we never get to be a part of it?" She let out a low, sexy growl that had me struggling to remember what we were talking about. "Look me in the eye and swear to me that this isn't some complex game that you and Bradford came up with to convince me to quit again."

I held her gaze. "I swear."

She pursed her lips and nodded. "Sorry. It's just that every time this feels like it might happen, it doesn't. I'm just frustrated."

So was I—on more than one front. I stepped closer. "I would never stand between you and something you want."

"I know." She searched my face. "And it's time for me to stop blaming others for what doesn't happen. I need to be more aggressive when it comes to going after what I want."

If she ever was toward me, I'd topple for sure. I was already close. The look in her eyes. The way my breathing deepened. I tried to remember why kissing her would be a bad idea, but damn it, I couldn't think of a single reason that outweighed how good being near her felt. I was attractive enough that having women blatantly want me wasn't unusual, but they didn't know me—not the way Katie did. Losing them never mattered, but Katie . . . I couldn't imagine my life without her in it.

Her tone was gentle when she said, "Last night my mother asked me where I want to be in five years—ten years."

"What did you say?"

"Here. I want to be in Driverton. I'd like a house. A husband. Some kids. And to be doing something I'm passionate about." Nothing could have dragged me away from her. In that moment there were no walls between us. "Where do you see yourself in the future? What do you want that you don't have? What brings you joy?"

The truth wasn't impressive, but I shared it anyway. "I don't ask myself those questions."

"You should. We deserve better than we've settled for."

"I'm good as I am."

"Are you?"

When I didn't maintain the claim that I was, she said, "I'm not *unhappy.* There's a lot about my life I don't want to change. I love working at Little Willie's because that's where everyone goes when they need help. I told my parents Little Willie's is the heart of Driverton and whatever happens in the future, I don't want to lose that."

"You won't."

"But I need more." She tilted her head to one side and gave me a long look. "Why did you choose to train with Bradford?"

I didn't like, nor was I willing to voice, the first answer that came to me. *You.* I shrugged.

"For Ollie?" When I didn't respond, she asked, *"For me?"*

I didn't have to tell her when she hit her mark. She'd always been able to read me too well. I shook my head, not in denial, but to try to clear nonsense from it. "No one wants to see you get hurt."

Her cheeks went pink, and I knew I'd made a mistake being too honest with her. "You agreed to train with Bradford then join the organization he runs with Cooper—to watch over me?" Tears were filling her eyes.

I'd never been good with emotional scenes. My voice was gruff when I said, "You know you're family to me. I don't see how this is surprising."

"It's not, really." She sniffed. "But it is beautiful."

"Don't read into it."

She nodded and sniffed again. "Right. Wouldn't want to think it meant anything. You'd do this for anyone."

I wouldn't, but I wasn't about to admit that either. Her

lips parted and I was so tempted. Instead, I reached up, grabbed the scrapbook, and handed it to her. "It's the damn scrapbook you made me when I graduated from high school. I don't even remember what's in it." That was a lie. I could remember every photo and every word she'd written beside them. I hadn't bought a yearbook because it included a lot of people I preferred to forget. Several towns had fed into our high school, and I wasn't popular with those from outside of Driverton. They saw me only as an angry kid who couldn't afford enough clothes to not wear the same ones each week. When neither of my parents returned for my graduation, I told myself I didn't care about them or anyone else.

I believed that until Katie handed me that fucking scrapbook. How she'd gotten photos of me with nearly everyone in town was mind boggling. Some were from when I was still in diapers, and some were more recent, but nearly everyone in town made it into that scrapbook and wrote a note near their photo. Peppered throughout the book were photos of Ollie, me, and Katie. I said, "You knew what that was as soon as you saw the corner of it."

Her smile was shameless. "I did."

"I don't know what game you're playing but count me out."

"There's no game." Some of the light left her expression. "This is as confusing for me as it is for you."

The silence was heavy with both sexual tension and mutual frustration. I felt cornered, turned on, and dangerously close to doing something stupid. "You and I are not on the same path, Katie. We don't want the same things. We don't look at life the same way. I don't think about five years from now—or ten. I live in today and fuck tomorrow."

"That's not—"

"It is true. I don't want a house—"

"Because you already have one."

"It's not mine." I didn't realize I'd raised my voice until I saw her eyes round.

"But—"

"Any day my parents wanted to, they could come back and boot me out of here. It's their names on the deed. None of this is mine."

Silence followed my bellowed words. Pity replaced the desire in her eyes and if I didn't care more for how she felt than how I did, I would have walked away.

After a bit, she said, "We wouldn't let them take it away from you."

That brought a twisted smile to my lips as I imagined Mrs. Williams on the front porch with her shotgun. Would Driverton fight for me? Without question. I didn't want that, though. They'd already been too good to me for far longer than I deserved. "I don't want to talk about this, Katie. The point I was trying to make is that you and I—"

She surged forward, went up onto her tiptoes, and brushed her lips over mine. I froze, unable to breathe. Or think. The scrapbook hit the floor. One of her hands slid around the back of my neck, urging my head lower and my restraint crumbled. I gripped her hips, pulling her against me. We kissed hungrily, our tongues circling, our breath mixing.

Nothing I'd experienced with others had prepared me for the intensity of our connection. We weren't yanking off each other's clothing and our hands remained chastely immobile, but an all-consuming fire raged through me until there was nothing beyond her and this moment.

One of her hands splayed on my chest between us, then moved lower to my rib cage. My cock strained, throbbed, would have roared for her to move her hand lower had it been able. Her other hand sifted through my hair, and I gave up on holding back. I lifted her, settling her so her legs were around my waist and both of my hands could cup her beautifully rounded ass. She moaned and writhed against me. I wanted to hear her moan again, to cry out my name as she begged me to keep going.

I needed more of her. I ran my hands upward to the waist of her jeans and yanked her shirt free from them. She gasped into our kiss then made a little sound from pleasure that echoed through me. My hands slid beneath the back of her shirt, savoring her smooth, warm back. With expertise, I whipped her shirt upward and off. There was no thought of stopping. Her bra hit the floor a mere second before I lifted her higher and claimed one of her breasts. Then the other. Both were absolute perfection.

Every woman was different when it came to what they liked and I prided myself on discovering exactly how to drive each of them wild, but with Katie I was incapable of my usual detachment. She wasn't a puzzle I was trying to figure out how to best please. She was a volcanic shockwave overtaking my entire being.

I helped her eager hands free me from my own shirt. Bare chest to bare chest, I kissed her shoulder, her arched neck, the delicate line of her jaw. She cupped my face, bringing my mouth once again to meet her hungry one.

"Hello?" Mrs. Williams called from the door at the top of the basement stairs. She must have let herself into the house. Shit. I quickly lowered Katie to her feet, tossed her clothing to her then grabbed my shirt and pulled it on as well. "Anyone here?"

We scrambled to tuck our shirts in. I ran my hands through Katie's hair to smooth it. She smiled and brushed some dirt off the top of mine. The heated look we exchanged was one I'd remember till the day I died—there was no going back to how we were before.

I picked up the scrapbook she'd dropped and inhaled deeply before saying, "Down here."

Katie's breath was as ragged as mine. Her face was flushed and unless there was time for both of us to get a cold shower from the hose, I couldn't imagine Mrs. Williams wouldn't know what we were up to.

Her footfall on the steps was distinctive and ominous.

Anger with myself had my hands fisting at my sides. Of all the people to find us that day, outside of Ollie, his mother was the worst-case scenario. I called out, "Katie, put that box down, I told you not to lift anything."

With an adorably conspiratorial smile, she said, "Stop bossing me around, Levi. I'm fine. It's a slight sprain, not a break. You're worse than Ollie, and it's starting to piss me off."

"Are you two fighting again?" Mrs. Williams asked as she came into view in the basement. "Levi, let the poor girl . . ." Her voice trailed away as she looked both of us over.

The air stilled.

She held Katie's gaze then mine.

I swallowed hard and waited. I loved Mrs. Williams. She'd been more of a mother to me than my own had ever been. She had my respect as well as my loyalty and I couldn't imagine ever not taking her side, but I would if whatever she said next was unkind to Katie.

Of all the wonderful traits Mrs. Williams had, keeping her thoughts to herself was not one of them. Much like I was, Katie seemed to be preparing herself for a lecture from the town's matriarch.

When none came it was almost worse.

Chapter Nine

Katie

I FELT NO shame as I stood there, shoulder to shoulder with Levi, waiting for Aunt Reana to express her displeasure at what she had clearly discerned was going on. Her lectures sometimes stung—but only when they were filled with truth we couldn't deny. We all knew she wanted the best for us— and from us. Disappointing her was something I tried to avoid even more than disappointing my parents.

I didn't see judgment in her eyes.

But nor did I see acceptance.

Remarkably, she was keeping whatever she felt about catching Levi and me in a compromising situation to herself. She spoke first. "Everette and Shelby came in to cover the dinner shift. When I heard you were cleaning out your basement, Levi, I thought I'd come by and see if you needed an extra set of hands." She looked over again. "How's your ankle, Katie?"

"Better today." I hugged the scrapbook to my stomach.

Her gaze was drawn to it and, for a second, I thought she was going to say something about it, but instead she looked around. "I hope you don't intend to just throw all of this away."

Levi shrugged. "It's time for it to go."

"I imagine it is," she said slowly. "Do you remember your grandmother, Levi?"

"Vaguely. I hadn't yet started school when she died."

Aunt Reana continued, "She was a good woman. Strong. Kind. When your grandfather died, she raised your mother on her own." She looked around the room again. "She knew as soon as your father rolled into town that he was trouble. There was no keeping your mother from him. So, she did her best to like him, especially after he became her son-in-law and you arrived. They lived here, all together, mostly in harmony because your grandmother would accept no less."

The sadness in Levi's eyes made me want to throw all caution to the wind and hug him right then and there but I remembered what Ollie had said about how I could cost Levi everything. I couldn't live with that.

Levi shook his head.

Aunt Reana's expression softened. "You were loved, Levi. And if your grandmother had lived, you would always have known that. She was the glue that held your mother together. When your grandmother died, your mother turned to your father for strength and that was more than he could handle. He started drinking. They started fighting. I can't tell you how many times I wanted to bury both of them in the field and raise you as my own."

I choked on an awkward laugh. Aunt Reana didn't hold back, that was for sure.

"Turns out you didn't have to do anything that extreme. They removed themselves from my life." Levi rubbed a hand over his eyes. After a pause, he added, "I appreciate what you're trying to do, Mrs. Williams, but I'm fine."

"Now listen here, Levi," Aunt Reana's tone turned harsh. "It's not all about you. I'm trying to say something and it's not easy. So, just give me a moment to get it right."

Levi and I exchanged a quick look. Aunt Reana was one of my favorite people in the world. I looked up to her, envied her ability to speak her mind, step in, and act when others hesitated. Her opinion of me mattered, but I'd hold my tongue if her lecture was about my behavior. I wouldn't be capable of doing that, though, if she said anything against Levi. If being with me put Levi on the outs with her, I'd stand with him—as he'd always stood with me.

"I've been worried about you and Ollie for a while." Aunt Reana said, "The older you boys have gotten, the more I've tried to let you sort things out on your own. Sometimes the hardest lessons to learn are the ones we have to, but I can't pretend I don't know—"

"I kissed Levi, he didn't kiss me. *I'm* the problem."

Levi groaned into his hand.

"Good to know." My aunt expelled an audible breath

after I cut her off. "But I'm talking about what Levi did for Ollie. I know Ollie checked into a rehab center. I've often wondered who your father might have been had he ever put down the bottle. Sober, he wasn't a mean man. Now neither you nor Ollie have a sober or drunken mean bone in your body, but I'm so glad you've both decided to start making better choices for yourselves."

Ollie's at a rehab center? My eyes flew to meet Levi's. *You could have told me.*

He answered me without speaking. *I couldn't. But maybe you didn't need to mention the kiss.*

I grimaced in wordless response. *Yeah, sorry.*

"Now about you two." Aunt Reana sighed. "I'm not here to judge how you conduct yourself in the privacy of your *basement.*" She said that, but there was a heavy amount of judgment in that last word.

Unlike me, Levi didn't appear nervous. He stood there, shoulders back, looking my aunt straight in the eye.

Normally my aunt folded in the face of nothing, but she softened at Levi's stance. "That's my niece, Levi, so you can stop looking ready to defend her honor. Do I think this is a good idea? No. Do I believe anything can stop it from happening? Also no."

"It was just a kiss," I said quickly.

Levi said firmly, "I would never hurt Katie."

"I know." My aunt lowered her arms. "Things sure are changing in Driverton lately. I suppose I'll just mind my business and hope for the best."

I laughed then stopped when she side-eyed me. "Sorry. I thought you were kidding."

Levi ducked his head and smiled.

Aunt Reana laid a hand on his arm. "Levi, look at me."

He raised his gaze to meet hers and it was only then that I saw how close to tears she was. "Thank you for watching out for Ollie."

"Of course," Levi said quietly.

"Promise me something."

I chewed my bottom lip and hoped it wasn't what Ollie had asked of both of us.

She gave his arm a squeeze. "Don't confuse anything stupid Ollie says when he finds out about this with how he'll always feel. Just like the two of you are—he's still figuring himself out. Give him the grace of forgiveness if he ends up needing some."

"I will," Levi said. "You know we never stay mad at each other long."

"You'd better not. Or I'll take a switch to both of your asses," Aunt Reana said, and I laughed again.

She released Levi's arm, put her hands on her hips and addressed me. "Do you have something you'd like to say, young lady?"

"Sorry, I was just imagining you chasing Levi with a stick and wondering if that would help him run faster."

Levi's mouth rounded, before twisting with a grin. "You heal up, then we'll have a rematch."

That had even my aunt chuckling. "You two . . . Levi, since I see you already have help, I'll head on home. Katie—"

"Yes?"

She gave me a quick hug. "I'm proud of the changes I'm seeing in you as well. Just—be kind to each other and be careful." With a wave over her shoulder, she made her way back up the basement steps.

Levi and I were alone again, neither one of us yet ready to meet the other's gaze. Should we discuss what happened? Pretend it hadn't?

My aunt seemed to think Levi and I were inevitable. Were we?

I thought back to what he'd been saying right before I kissed him, and embarrassment flooded in. He hadn't been asking me out or even flirting with me. He'd been explaining why nothing between us was possible. "I'm sorry."

He cleared his throat. "You have nothing to be sorry for."

Looking down at the scrapbook in my arms, I shared my greatest fear. "Just so you know, I can handle not training with Bradford. If Ollie ever fired me—for real, not his every other week idle threat—I'd survive and find another job. But I can't imagine us not being friends."

"I feel the same."

"I shouldn't have kissed you." Disappointment swept over me when he nodded.

"I didn't exactly fight you off, but we should spend less

time alone together until things go back to normal."

"Yes. Getting back to normal. That's the goal." I brought my gaze up to meet his.

The look in his eyes gutted me. He was determined to do the right thing and protect me. But was that what I wanted? Needed?

"It has to be."

Did it?

Why? Because he couldn't be faithful? Because both he and Ollie feared I wouldn't matter more to him than the sex partners he currently sought?

I already did.

He'd proven how much he cared about me again and again—for as long as I could remember. A little voice in my heart whispered a possibility that at first seemed implausible, but the more I mulled it, the more I wanted it to be true.

What if . . . *what if* he didn't feel anything for those other women because I already had his heart? I'd told myself that the sabbatical I'd taken from dating after my last relationship was due to how badly it had ended. The bruises on my face had faded after a few weeks, but my distrust of men in general had lingered.

Except with Levi.

Looking back at that time, he was the one who'd come to see me when I'd been too ashamed to leave my house. He'd brought makeup to cover my bruises and stupid stories that had me laughing even when I hadn't been sure I ever would again.

He made a sound deep in his throat. "We have to be on the same page about this."

Yes, we did. "Can I ask you something?"

His expression said he knew it was a bad idea to agree but did so anyway. "Sure."

"It's been five years since I've had sex."

He coughed. "That's not a question."

I continued, "I'm getting to one. Besides, I'm not telling you anything you don't know."

"I don't let myself think about it. Could you get to the point?"

"What if . . . Hear me out . . . Our lives feel like they're out of our control, but really, everything that happened had to for us to be where we are."

"What?"

In a gush, I said, "Have you ever considered celibacy?"

A flush darkened his cheeks and he inhaled sharply. "No."

My heart started racing. "They say it can really help a person clear their head of distractions."

"Katie—"

"I've gone years without sex, and it hasn't killed me. All I'm suggesting is you go a few months. Hooking up with women you don't want to see again is a habit, no different than drinking was, that you've used to make yourself feel better, but it doesn't, does it?"

"Okay, it's time for you to go."

"You know I'm right."

"Hand me the scrapbook and I'll walk you out." He held out a hand to receive it.

Reluctantly, I passed it to him. "Promise me you'll think about it."

He led the way out of his basement. Feeling slightly ridiculous, I followed him. Thankfully, I hadn't told anyone about how my feelings for Levi were changing.

I wasn't ready to field questions about how things were going.

Great.

I kissed him.

He told me we shouldn't do that again.

I recommended he stop sleeping with random women.

He asked me to leave.

We're making real progress.

Once inside my car, I rolled down the window and said, "What's the worst thing that could happen?"

"You and I accidentally fuck," he said gruffly before turning and walking away.

I tried to see that as a horrible possibility but couldn't. Giving in to an impulse, I called out, "Fine. If it's good enough for you, it's good enough for me. There are a lot of single men out there and maybe it's time I sample a few."

He stopped mid-stride. "You don't mean that, Katie."

"I do. You're the first person I've kissed in—forever. No wonder I pounced on you. But don't worry, I will direct my needs in a more receptive direction."

He stormed back to my car window. "Stop."

I threw my hands up. "You're the one who said you'd be at my wedding, celebrating me marrying someone else. How am I supposed to do that if I don't get out there and—"

"You win. I won't fuck anyone. Okay? No one. Just my hand. Unless that's off limits too."

"Is this a bad time?" a deep male voice asked from the other side of the driveway.

Levi spun toward him. I slunk deep into the driver seat. After taking several deep breaths, I said, "Hey, Bradford."

"I heard Levi was cleaning out his basement and thought he might need some help, so I jogged over." There really were no secrets in Driverton. "Feeling any better?"

Even though I was mortified, I forced a bright smile. "I can walk a little on it, but no running for me for a bit."

"It's good to let it heal before you push yourself," Bradford said abruptly. "I'm sorry that happened to you. It wouldn't have had I . . ."

"It's okay," I assured him. Relationships were complicated.

"It's not, but it won't happen again." He flexed his shoulders. "Joanna would like to train alongside the two of you if you're still interested."

My eyes flew to Levi's. *Please still want to.*

He was not happy with me, but he nodded. "I am."

"Me too," I said.

"Good. Both of you come to my house tomorrow after the breakfast shift."

I glanced at Levi. "I should be fine to work it alone."

"Then I'll finish the fence," Levi said. I'd expected him to still offer to help at Little Willie's, but that wouldn't have fit with his plan of spending less time with me.

After a somewhat awkward pause I said, "Bradford, I'm heading home. Would you like me to drop you off on my way?"

"No, but thanks."

"Okay." I got back into my car and started it. "So, I'll see you both tomorrow."

Bradford nodded.

Levi didn't say a word, but he didn't have to. I knew he'd be there.

It was impossible to contain the smile that spread across my face as I drove away. Levi could claim whatever he wanted to, but he'd just agreed to something he refused to consider with other women—exclusivity.

After one kiss.

Not bad.

Chapter Ten

Levi

M Y THOUGHTS WERE still jumbled as I watched Katie drive away. What the hell had I just agreed to?

Bradford rubbed a hand over the back of his neck as he tried and failed to conceal his amusement. "Want to talk about it?"

"No."

"Thank God."

"I do have a lot of shit to load into the back of my truck, though."

"That's why I'm here."

We made several trips from the basement to the truck, carrying cardboard boxes, plastic storage containers and trash bags full of whatever I'd decided years earlier I no longer wanted to look at. Finally throwing it away felt as if I were shedding a weight I'd carried for too long.

After we determined the truck bed wouldn't safely hold another layer, we secured the items with bungee cords and stood back to assess our work. "Looks like it'll hold," I said.

"At least as far as Everette's house," Bradford answered. "He and Shelby offered to sort through it. If they find anything they think you—"

"They won't. I should have gotten rid of all of it a long time ago. Thanks. I can do the rest tomorrow."

"Hey."

I stopped, turned toward Bradford, and waited.

He said, "What you said to me about Joanna not wanting to live in only one of my lives—that helped me see that leaving Driverton wouldn't have changed anything."

"I'm glad. You seem like you have something really good with her."

"I do." He looked so uncomfortable I felt a little sorry for him. I didn't like talking about my personal shit either. "Do you know what's the hardest part of what I do?"

I grimaced. "Shooting people?"

It was difficult to tell if he was joking when he said, "No, that's actually not that difficult. The struggle for me has always been to not absorb the pain of everyone we don't get to in time. Prior to meeting Joanna, I was eighty percent rage and twenty percent guilt. I was doing what I considered the right thing, but not always for the right reasons."

"That's understandable." I knew enough about his life before Joanna to have a pretty good idea why he might have lost his way. Sometimes rage was justified.

"You were dealt a shitty hand," he said.

"It is what it is."

"Your parents obviously had issues."

I frowned. "If you've got something you want to say, Bradford, just say it."

He made a frustrated sound. "Whatever was wrong with them, don't take it in, don't make it yours."

"Everette said you gave him a pep talk when you started working with him. Is this how it went?"

"No. He sees good in everyone and imagines himself a hero. I had to explain to him how that might one day get him killed."

"Yeah."

"Trust is key when working with someone on the types of jobs I take on." Bradford folded his arms across his chest. "You could pass every physical and mental test I throw your way, but I need to know what your motivation for working with me is before I agree to let you join us. You're not in it for the glory."

"Nope."

"I haven't seen you accept a dime of financial help you've been offered."

I shrugged. Money or my lack of it had never mattered much to me.

He continued, "If Katie is the only reason you're training with me, that'll be a problem. Distractions like that make a person a liability."

"Bullshit." Rising to my full height, I growled, "Tell me

you'd let Joanna go into any battle without you at her side. Look me right in the eye and say it." When he didn't, I added, "No? That's what I thought. If I'm a liability, you're one as well. I'll cover your ass and risk my life to rescue anyone I'm sent to, but when shit goes down, I'll save Katie first—every single time. If you wouldn't do the same for Joanna, you're not the man I think you are."

His eyes narrowed but he lowered his arms. "Joanna would tell me not to, but I'd rather live with her anger and my guilt than without her."

I relaxed my stance as well. "Then you understand why I wasn't upset when you said you wouldn't work with us. I don't have too much I care about but . . ."

"You don't have to explain. Joanna does this thing with each new horse she brings to the rescue. She asks them what they've learned from life and what they'd like to learn from her. I used to tease her about it because—well, they can't answer her, but somehow they do. They always do."

I tensed as what he seemed to be saying sunk in. "I'm not a rescue."

"Maybe not, but I'm going to help you anyway."

"What are you talking about, Bradford?"

"Tell me about this promise you were making to her when I arrived."

"No."

"That was a hard line for her to ask you to toe, but a good place to start if things are getting serious between the two of you."

"Bradford, respectfully, anything that does or doesn't happen between Katie and me is none of your business." I felt I needed to also say, "We're just friends, though."

For a man whose appearance might put the devil himself on guard, Bradford appeared unsure of how to proceed. "Normally, I wouldn't have gotten even this involved, but the talk Joanna and I had after you left our house would have taken significantly longer to get to had you not intervened. You made me face some truths I didn't want to."

"I'm glad it worked out, but—"

"Friends don't promise not to fuck other people. Whether you want to admit it or not, you're already in a relationship with her. The question you need to ask yourself is why is that a problem?"

Shaking my head, I searched for an answer to his question. "I'm okay with not having anything. This house isn't mine. I support myself with odd jobs and what I grow on this farm. Small savings. No plan. What do I have to offer a woman like Katie? She deserves so much more."

"So, anyone with money in the bank would be perfect for her. She wants a huge house to impress her friends, expensive clothing, a new car every year."

"No, that's not Katie."

"What does she want?"

"To be part of something important. To raise a family here in Driverton of all places. She'd even like to keep working at Little Willie's because she likes to help people and that's where people go when they need something."

"What's stopping you from being someone who could share that with her?"

I looked at the boxes of my parents' crap then rubbed a hand down my face. "I don't know if I have what it takes to stay—with her or anyone."

He let out an audible breath.

With a shrug, I said, "Ollie's my best friend and even he doesn't believe I'd be good for her. Katie has been so kind to me her entire life. Even when she followed Ollie and me around, she was always looking out for me—always making sure I was okay. When my parents left, I shut down. I fucked up and kept fucking up. Maybe I wanted to see if I could drive everyone else away too. Katie was out there, going door to door, practically campaigning for me. I was too proud to tell anyone I needed help, but she made sure I got it." I swallowed hard. "You don't take advantage of someone like that. You don't lead them on or make them promises you can't keep."

"Did you lie to her when you said you wouldn't see other women?"

"No. I meant it."

"It'll just be a struggle for you."

I sighed. "Honestly? Lately, there isn't anyone I'm interested in anyway."

After a moment, he said, "I understand, and I do have

something I can teach you."

I frowned without meeting his gaze.

He continued, "When you remove the option of quitting, your brain no longer sees it as a possibility and something inside you shifts. When you can endure more, your focus increases and unexpected solutions materialize. Death is an outcome none of us can avoid, but we have influence over how and when it happens. I see a lot of good in you, Levi, but it's sloppy and confined to those you deem worthy of it. Train with me, really train, and I'll show you that when loyalty, courage, discipline, respect, and honor become an integral part of you—nothing from your past can hold you back from getting what you want."

"You don't know me at all if you think I have huge dreams I'm holding back on sharing. I am happily living day to day, and you can call that sloppy, but it's gotten me this far."

Bradford rubbed his knuckles on one side of his chin. "Everyone wants something. Everette was looking for a way to feel better about himself. Ollie needs a win to boost his confidence. Katie seeks to belong. What motivates *you*? What would you be willing to risk everything for?"

I could have said Katie again, but he already knew that. Instead, I said, "I want none of what you've brought to Driverton to hurt the people I care about."

"I can work with that," Bradford said. "And give you the skills to protect them if trouble ever does find them." He held out his hand for me to shake. "Lesson one: becoming comfortable with the uncomfortable, persevering past pain."

I joked as I shook it. "Why do I feel that this will involve finishing fencing all of your fields?"

He barked out a laugh, then a slow smile spread across his face, "Because you're a smart man who puts up fencing better than anyone I've hired in the past."

"I'll do it, but your ass had better be out there sweating every day as well. You can't be married to a horsewoman and not be able to properly install a fence."

Chapter Eleven

Katie

MID-AFTERNOON, THREE WEEKS later, Joanna and I were speed walking on side-by-side treadmills at the gym in her house while watching instructional videos on the art of hostage negotiation. Daily circuit training with light weights, yoga and low-impact aerobic activities had proven surprisingly effective at toning and strengthening my body. I hadn't considered myself out of shape, but not only did my clothing fit better, I had more energy and felt better in general.

"How is Levi doing?" I slowed the treadmill. It bothered me to ask a question I should know the answer to. Before Ollie had left, I'd seen Levi daily. I'd assumed that training with Bradford would mean Levi and I would spend even more time together, but I'd hardly seen him.

No more car rides together. No time alone at all. He'd made sure of that.

Every day, Levi and Bradford put up fences and trained

on Bradford's farm while I did breakfast shifts at Little Willie's. Aunt Reana covered lunch and Levi dinner.

Levi had said we needed to spend less time together to let things cool down. Was it working for him? I hoped not, because it was having the opposite effect on me. I missed him so much I ached.

Driverton was a small enough town that I could have forced my presence on him, but as much as I wanted to see him, I also cared about him. If he wanted us to return to being friends and no more—that's what I'd do.

Somehow.

Joanna slowed her pace and used a towel to wipe sweat from her forehead. "Levi and Bradford are still beating the snot out of each other. They call it sparring, but I've told Bradford that's not how I want to learn."

I made a pained face. "Me neither. I don't remember Everette saying he and Bradford ever got into it like that."

"Probably because Bradford sees Everette as more of a little brother."

That was easy enough to believe. Despite towering over everyone in town, Everette had a golden retriever personality. "And Levi?" My protective nature kicked in. I wasn't about to say it, but in my opinion, Levi's training should be easier than Everette's had been since Levi was doing it for *me*.

"Bradford said he has the grit of a Navy SEAL and real leadership potential. He's pushing Levi hard because he knows he can take it. I was concerned when I saw Levi with a split lip and swollen cheek, but then I found marks on Bradford." Joanna chuckled. "Bradford is used to being the toughest dog in a fight, but Levi doesn't back down. With all the working out and physical combat training they're doing, Bradford is creating a worthy adversary for himself. And Levi isn't complaining."

The idea that Levi could stand up to Bradford had my face warming and my thoughts filling with memories of his kiss, his hands, the feel of his skin against mine. Although I hadn't been alone with him since that day in his basement, I'd seen him in passing. He was standing up straighter, looking people in the eye more, and overall seemed more comfortable in his own skin—despite the bruises. "Levi always did stand his ground. I used to worry about him when we were in school. After his parents left, he got into so many fights."

"Teenagers can be cruel."

"They sure can be, especially when they can't control you. Our high school was a regional one, serving several towns. Levi hung out mostly with the kids from Driverton. If someone had a problem with one of them, they had a problem with Levi as well. He's never been able to not get involved when he sees someone in trouble."

Joanna stepped off her treadmill. "I can see why you love him."

"I do love him. I've known him my whole life and he's one of my best friends. *Or was . . .*" I stumbled, then stepped off as well. How much was too much to share was still something I was figuring out when it came to Joanna.

"I wish you'd stop that." She tossed me a fresh towel that I caught and wrapped around the back of my neck.

"What?" I was grateful for everything I was learning from Bradford and the opportunities that might come from it. His wife was the last person I wanted to offend.

"Seeing me as someone you can't talk honestly to." She sighed. "If I tell you something, could you keep it between the two of us?"

"Absolutely."

Retrieving her water bottle from the front of her treadmill, she swirled the water in it as she seemed to choose her next words. "I had a selfish reason for wanting to train while you were."

I waited and tried not to entertain any nefarious possibilities.

She continued, "My best friends are married and traveling all over the world with their husbands. I don't want that life, but I miss them. I love what I do. I love that Bradford is following a calling that few have the fortitude for. But sometimes, especially when I'm waiting for him to return from a job, I wish I had a friend I could pop in on and not have to explain how I feel—she'd just know. We'd share a tub of popcorn, watch corny old movies, and I'd leave feeling better even if we never talked about what I was afraid of. Do you have a friend like that?"

Levi. "I don't know anymore."

"I know you see me as Bradford's wife, but I'm also a good listener if you ever need one."

I searched her face. She was only a few years older than I was, but came across as someone who had it all figured out while I was still struggling. Everette said Bradford had chosen to move to Driverton with his wife because they wanted to be part of a close-knit community. Was it possible Joanna and I had more in common than I'd thought? "I love popcorn and old movies."

Joanna smiled.

I smiled back.

And a new level of friendship was born.

I lifted my previously injured ankle and rolled it in the air. "Shelby asked me to join Everette and her on their morning runs and I've been telling her I can't yet, but the truth is I don't enjoy running anymore. I prefer our walks and yoga."

Joanna wrinkled her nose. "I like learning about hostage negotiation and escape techniques, but I don't actually want to learn combat skills." Joanna chuckled. "I want to be part of what Bradford does, but if there's a PT test at the end of this, I'm afraid I won't pass it. Whenever he tries to show me self-defense moves, we just end up having sex. I'm failing his training program."

Laughter gurgled in my chest. "I'm sure he doesn't see it that way."

Smiling, she confessed, "He suggested a high protein/low carb muscle-building diet in preparation for strength training, but I have an addiction to Manju's lemon pastries and stash some in the fridge in the barn."

"Shelby offered to show me how to lift weights and scale walls. I told her God wouldn't have made those weights so heavy if he wanted them off the floor. And the wall? I'd rather find a door or gate and pick it than Spiderman-scale it. You should have seen her face."

"Great minds think alike." We shared a laugh then she sobered. "All I really wanted was to be included."

I was coming to some realizations myself. "I just want to make a difference. I like helping people and solving puzzles. If it paid better, working at Little Willie's would be my dream job." I brought my hands up to cover my eyes. "That's pathetic, isn't it? My friends all went to college and moved away. They think I'm wasting my time here. My parents agree. And here I am perfectly okay with remaining mediocre . . ."

She touched my arm gently. "Stop. That's not how I see you at all."

I lowered my hands and met her gaze.

She added, "You've chosen to stay and do something you love. Okay, so it's not financially lucrative, but have you considered that Driverton and Little Willie's might need you? I've seen you wait on tables of people who brought their own lunch because they couldn't afford to buy a meal and you didn't make them feel any different for it. I've also witnessed how you connect people in need with those who can help them. You do it so naturally and seamlessly, people take it for granted. I bet you don't realize that many of those connections wouldn't happen if you weren't there to facilitate them."

I shrugged. "All I'm doing is what Ollie's father always did. He had a way of making everyone feel valued."

"There is nothing mediocre about bringing happiness to people. You already make a difference."

I wanted to believe that. "As nice as that all sounds, I can't live above my parents' garage forever. To move out and get a place of my own I'll need a job that pays better."

Joanna nodded. "I'll talk to Bradford. Few things are all or nothing. What he values most in his team is honesty and loyalty. Instead of trying to be like him, let's take the strengths we already have and use them to support what he does."

"I'm a good shot and am getting really good at picking locks."

"You're also very easy to talk to."

"Thanks."

"Bradford will need a community liaison—someone people trust."

Hope lit in me. "I'd love that role. People already come to Little Willie's when they want to know what's going on."

"You'd be in charge of ensuring the people of Driverton

feel heard and supported. If someone has an issue that can't be solved in the regular manner, Bradford and I would like to help out discreetly."

"You mean the way everyone in Driverton received overdue government payouts for an old land issue no one remembers happening? Funds that oddly enough were just enough to pay off their mortgages?"

Joanna wrinkled her nose. "That wasn't us."

I pinned her with a look. "Well, it wasn't the government."

She seemed reluctant to acknowledge that someone had, then sighed and spoke in a conspiratorial voice. "Bradford started off with nothing, but some in his circle were born into wealth . . ."

"Like Clay Landon, Cooper's brother?"

"Yes."

"Why would he pay off the debts of people he hardly knows?"

She shrugged. "Clay is . . . complicated. A lot of people dream of being wealthy because they think it would solve all of their problems. They don't understand that it can bring about all sorts of new ones."

My thoughts wandered to Levi and how vulnerable he'd sounded when he'd admitted he owned nothing. Did he think any of us cared about whose name was on his house or what he had in the bank? I hated to think he might.

In a soft tone, Joanna said, "You've got that sad look on

your face again. Thinking about Levi?"

My head snapped back, and I almost denied it, but then chose the harder path of the truth. "Yes. I miss him." My chest tightened. "He's doing everything he can to avoid me."

"Did you argue?"

"Worse." I looked away then met her gaze. "We kissed."

"Oh." She pursed her lips. "So, that's it."

"That's it."

"Bradford told me Ollie is against the two of you getting together. Why?"

"Levi has a history of not staying long with one woman. Ollie's worried he'll hurt me."

"What do you think?"

"I don't know. He's always been wonderful to me, but on the other hand, he's practically hiding from me right now and that's a first. I go back and forth between imagining I might be the reason Levi's never been serious about another woman . . . and thinking I'm delusional and Ollie is right."

Joanna nodded slowly. "People had their doubts about Bradford at first. He's been through more than most could survive and has the scars to prove it, but I've never met anyone more loving. Not everyone gets to see that side of him and I'm okay with that. I know who he is with me and why he is who he is with others. Coming to Driverton has been good for us because his two lives overlap here, and I am finally able to show him that I accept all of him—not just the man he becomes for me. He doesn't need to protect me from the man I love."

He doesn't need to protect me from the man I love.

Hugging my arms around myself, I weighed those words. My feelings for Levi were in a painful jumble. *I can't lose him. He's pulling away to protect me.*

What if we can't go back to how we were?

Where will that leave us?

Nowhere?

Joanna broke into my thoughts. "Levi obviously cares about you. You care about him. Things will work out the way they're meant to."

How they're meant to? I sighed. I was so turned around I didn't know what I was hoping that would be anymore.

Chapter Twelve

Levi

A FEW WEEKS later, I was on my tractor, tilling a field that would soon be ready for a second crop that season. I was in the best shape of my life, had learned how to effectively protect myself with and without weapons, and knew more than I'd ever thought I'd want to about explosives.

Bradford brought out a couple of his ex-Special Forces friends and not only had me spar against them but challenged my sharpshooting skills as well as my ability to problem solve under pressure. I must have held my own because both men left contact information along with offers of insanely high-paying security positions with their businesses. Although the money was tempting, I had no desire to leave Driverton.

When Bradford appeared on the edge of the field, I cut the tractor's engine. He'd run rather than driven over, which didn't surprise me at all. No one stayed in the shape he did without constantly pushing himself to remain there.

I hopped down from my tractor and made my way over to him. "If you're here to talk, there are a few boards on my back porch that are rotting out. We'll pull them up and nail down some replacements."

He nodded and fell into step beside me. "It's been twenty-four hours since you were offered jobs that most people in your position wouldn't have turned down. Any regrets?"

We stopped at one of my sheds and began to gather some tools. "Not one. I told you what I wanted to gain from my time with you."

He accepted a crowbar from me. "The skills to protect the town."

It wasn't a question, so I didn't feel the need to respond. I led the way to my house. Always more of a doer than a talker, I nodded for him to pry up one of the rotted boards while I gathered the replacements.

We'd been working for a while before he spoke. "Ollie's doing so well he's not in a rush to return. You two still in touch?"

"We were talking every day when he needed the support. He has a lot going on now, so it's been a bit since I've heard from him. That's good though. He needed to go away to find his footing."

"You okay if he decides not to come back?"

I paused from removing a nail from a crossbeam. That wasn't a possibility I'd allowed myself to consider, but I shrugged in the face of it. "People are going to do what people are going to do."

Bradford pried another board free. "You're probably better off without him."

I tensed, ready to jump to the defense of my best friend, but I'd spent the last several weeks holding back instinctive reactions to allow myself the time for clarity of thought. Assessing a situation quickly and calmly was Bradford's number one secret to survival. Rather than focusing on how I felt, I questioned his motivation for saying something he knew would piss me off. Unlike how he dealt with adversaries, Bradford often led with a light punch when he wanted to wake a friend up for something more intense. This wasn't about Ollie. "Did something happen to Katie?"

"No."

Then whatever it was, I could handle it. I let out a breath of relief.

He cleared his throat. "Ollie shouldn't have told you to stay away from her."

I returned my attention to replacing an old board with a new one. "I wouldn't have promised to if I didn't think it was what's best for her."

"There was a time when I would have agreed with you. I thought you'd crumble as soon as I started to really push you."

"Thanks?" Not all compliments were easy to hear.

"I intentionally made things miserable for you."

"Okay."

"I needed to see what it would take for you to quit."

He hadn't told me anything I didn't already know so I kept working.

"But you rose to each challenge." He continued, "Loyal. Smart. Not motivated by money. Not afraid of pain. You're exactly the type I want on my team . . ."

"But?" His tone implied there was one.

"Trust is key in what we do. Secrets can erode that."

"My life is an open book—ask anyone in town and they'll tell you all my business."

"We need to talk about your parents."

"Ask me anything."

He made a sound deep in his throat. "Clay located them."

The hammer I'd been holding slipped from my hand and fell to the dirt below the deck. Shit. Slowly, I dropped to my knees and tried to reach it but couldn't. When I sat back on my heels, I expelled the breath that had nearly choked me. "How are they?"

"No longer alive. Sorry."

My empty hands fisted on my thighs. "How?"

"Boating accident. They were in—"

"No," I said firmly and stood. "I don't care."

"I feel that you should know—"

I raised both hands between us, cutting him off. *My parents are dead. Dead.* None of the feelings I would have expected to experience materialized. Grief? No. Relief? None. A little anger would have been welcome. Anything, really.

If only I could breathe . . .

On autopilot, I walked to the shed to look for another hammer. My abrupt movements knocked a mason jar of nails over and I cursed as they bounced off the floor in every direction.

"There was no good way to tell you," Bradford said gruffly beside me.

"I'm fine." Without looking away from my wall of tools, I growled, "They've been dead to me for a long time."

"Do you want me to call someone?"

"No."

After a moment, he said, "I should have led with this, but you're already part of my team. You're in."

I let out a pained laugh behind the hand I rubbed down my face. My voice was thick with sarcasm. "Good, I was worried about that."

"You're going to be okay, Levi."

"I never said I wouldn't be." I spun on my heel to face him. "Don't you have somewhere you need to be? Like, anywhere else?"

"You should call Ollie."

"So I can be his excuse to start drinking again? No thanks." It was a dick thing to say, but I didn't want to be in this conversation. Not with him. Not with anyone.

"Everette or Cooper—"

"I appreciate the thought, but I don't need anyone. What I need to do is finish the porch before it's too dark to and I work faster alone."

"Understood, but . . ."

I shot him an annoyed look that he answered with a nod before turning and walking away.

Chapter Thirteen

Katie

THE SUN HAD set, and the air had begun to cool by the time I found myself standing on Levi's porch with a bag of groceries. His car wasn't in the driveway, but that didn't deter me. Aunt Reana had called me when Levi had shown up at Little Willie's in an unusually foul mood. She'd wanted to know if we'd had an argument.

We'd have to have spoken recently to have done that.

When he didn't respond to my text, I'd called Joanna, heard the news Bradford had given Levi, and my heart broke for him. A little voice in me whispered: *If he wanted me here, he would have asked me to be.*

No. Levi was too proud for that. No wonder he was grumpy. Rather than facing what he was feeling, he was out there trying to convince himself he wasn't devastated.

A part of him had held on to the slim hope that his parents would one day return. This must feel like he'd lost them all over again.

Joanna warned me that Levi didn't seem ready to talk to anyone, but I wasn't just anyone. I was the one he'd comforted when I'd felt lost and had thought I'd wanted to be alone. With that last thought bolstering me, I opened his front door and walked inside. Had our roles been reversed, he wouldn't have given me the choice to hide and wallow.

Besides, I'd brought steak and all the ingredients for my home-made macaroni and cheese with bacon just the way he liked it. It was his favorite meal and, I hoped, the perfect way to remind him that he wasn't alone.

Balancing the bag of food on one hip, I flipped on the living room light. Levi's decorating style could best be described as non-existent. He lived like a squatter who expected the homeowner to return soon and was prepared to leave with a few moments' notice. The walls were bare as were most of the shelves. One built-in bookcase displayed an assortment of photos of him with Ollie, Everette, Cooper, and me over the years. I picked up one of just me in my cap and gown on the day I graduated from high school. Replacing the photo, I told myself that no matter what had happened between us or how awkward things might be, we were family and needed to work it through.

There was only one item on the shelf below—the scrapbook I'd made for him. I laid one hand on it. My parents had thought that having everyone in town add to the book and write messages to him was a little over the top, but it had been what he'd needed back then. A younger me had plowed ahead, trusting my heart when it came to him, and I'd been right.

What did it tell me he needed now?

Me.

I hugged the bag of groceries to me then turned and walked to the kitchen. Time away from Levi should have filled me with doubt, but his decision to avoid me was based on the misconception that he couldn't stay . . . but he'd always been there for me.

Always.

What if . . . what if he wasn't afraid he'd hurt me by moving on . . . what if he was afraid *I'd* leave *him*? Once that possibility had come to me it had been impossible to shake.

I turned on the light in his modest kitchen, placed the bag of food on the counter, and began to unpack it. Whether we remained friends or became more, I would show him I wasn't going anywhere. He needed to know he was loved.

I texted Aunt Reana: **Send Levi home.**

She answered: **You know what's bugging him?**

I do.

It took her a moment to respond. **You're old enough to know what you're doing. I'd tell you to be careful but Levi's a good boy, even if he doesn't see it.**

I see it.

I know you do and that's why no matter how worried I am, I won't show up unannounced again—not until after the babies come, anyway.

I choked in surprise and then almost claimed that was an

impossibility, but I didn't know what the future held for Levi and me. It was clear, though, that Ollie was wrong about his mother taking my side over Levi's. Maybe because she also knew what it was like to lose family and start over, but in her heart, she had two sons.

What was in *my* heart?

I was still struggling with that question. *What's the difference between loving someone and being in love with them?*

Just lust?

Didn't that fade?

I brewed a pot of coffee, seasoned the steaks, and brought water to a boil for elbow pasta. Cooking was something I'd always enjoyed. I propped my phone on the counter and sang along to my favorite songs while prepping the cheese. Being in Levi's house felt right on a deeper level than I'd expected. It was insanely easy to imagine living with him and raising a family.

I shook my head. *We're friends first.*

And maybe never more.

What's important is that we don't ruin what we already have.

"What are you doing?" Levi asked from the door of the kitchen.

I forced confidence into my smile. "Making you your favorite meal."

The way he filled the doorway took my breath away. His shoulders were wider, his arms bulged beneath the sleeves of a shirt that used to be loose on him. I couldn't stop my gaze from dipping lower to appreciate how the jeans I'd seen him in for years strained to contain how muscular his thighs had become. If he kept working out, would he burst from his clothing like the Hulk? I bit my bottom lip.

He frowned. "I'm not hungry."

I wished I weren't. *Damn.* "You're welcome."

His nostrils flared. "Who told you?"

My pride warred with my love for him. I leaned back against the counter. "*You* should have."

He shook his head in frustration as he closed the distance between us. "I didn't because I knew you'd do this."

"What? Come over because I care about you? Oh, how horrible of me." He was so close I could feel the heat of him. The urge to run my hands up that flat stomach of his was nearly irresistible.

"I can't do this, Katie."

"Do what? Talk? You need to. If you bottle it up—"

He dipped his head and claimed my mouth with his. I bunched his shirt in my hands and held on tight. He moaned against my lips, and I parted them for him without resistance. Shamelessly writhing against his hardness, I gave myself over to my hunger for him.

Time apart hadn't lessened the lure of him. If anything, it had fanned the fire of desire. His hands settled on my hips, locking me against his bulging cock. Our mouths opened wider, and his tongue became deliciously forceful.

Still, it wasn't enough. I felt out of control and craved

the same from him. Sliding one of my hands between us and downward, I began to rub him through his clothing.

"I want you so bad," he growled then kissed his way down my jaw. Panting, I arched my neck, eagerly giving him access to more of me. Our movements became less and less gentle. His large, rough hands yanked my shirt up and over my head. My bra followed.

I wanted him to rush, but he took his time kissing my collarbone, my shoulders, and finally the upper curve of my breasts. I dug my nails into his still-clothed back and begged him not to stop.

When his mouth closed over one of my breasts, I melted in his arms. He hungrily adored my puckered nipple, sucking it, gently tugging at it with his teeth. Impatiently I undid the front of his jeans and slid the front of his boxers down, releasing his thick, hard cock. God, if he felt this good in my hands how would he feel inside me?

Frantically, wildly, we began to rip away each other's clothing until we stood there, bare skin to bare skin, gasping for air.

"Katie," he murmured against my hair. "You deserve so much better than me."

Digging my hands into his hair, I pulled his face around and kissed him.

He returned the kiss then raised his head, his fingertips brushing over the tips of my breasts as if they were a treasure he was afraid his strong hands might break. "I can have sex and feel nothing for the person the next day."

I froze as his words washed over me. He was being honest with me. Was I being as honest with myself? Could I really handle being just friends if we did this?

He closed his eyes briefly, then met my gaze again. Nothing could have torn me from him when he looked down at me with the same jumble of confused feelings I felt whenever around him. "But I already feel too much for you."

I released the breath I had unknowingly been holding. "That doesn't sound like a bad thing."

He blinked a few times quickly. "Katie, I feel like I'm drowning. I won't take you down with me."

I threw my arms around him and gave him a hug with my very soul. "Friends don't let friends drown alone." Okay, that had sounded better in my head than it did aloud. "You know what I mean. I'm not going anywhere."

He buried his face in my neck and his arms closed around me. "Why are you so stubborn?"

Cheek to chest, I mumbled, "If I was hurting, you'd be right at my side making sure I was okay. That's all I want to do."

He coughed. "Then why are we naked?"

I tipped my head back and the smile in his eyes brought one to my lips. "Full disclosure, comforting you might not be *all* I want to do."

"Thank God," he said with a deep, sexy chuckle. Nodding toward his still fully erect cock, he said, "He'd be more than a little disappointed."

"Wouldn't want that."

His expression tightened. "I spent all day wondering why I wasn't the least bit sad that my parents are dead. Now I'm asking myself why after five minutes with you I feel like I'm falling apart."

Cupping his face between my hands, I spoke from my heart. "Because you know you're safe with me. Just like I know I am with you."

He inhaled deeply. "I can't fuck this up. I can't lose you."

Was he saying what I thought he was saying? My body shuddered as I weathered the disappointment. "I understand."

His arms tightened around me and he lifted me off my feet with ease. "I don't think you do." He turned off the fire beneath the boiling water.

"Then explain it to me," I said breathlessly.

"Oh, I will. All night. I promise."

Heat flared through me. He was a man who didn't make promises lightly, but when he did, he kept them. There wasn't a lick of fear in me as he carried me naked through his house and up the stairs to his bedroom. Anticipation increased with every step, every jostle of my breasts against his chest.

I nearly wept at how tenderly he placed me on his bed. For a long moment he stood there, cock waving in the air, simply looking down at me. With anyone else I would have felt vulnerable and exposed, but all I felt was wanted and grateful. His gaze was a caress of its own. In that moment he was both the friend he'd always been as well as the lover I'd fantasized he could be.

"So damn beautiful," he said in a thick voice.

I looked him over, every beefed-up, gorgeous inch of him. "Yes."

He crawled onto the bed and positioned himself above me. The warmth of him, scent of him, filled my senses. I snaked my fingers through his hair and pulled his face down to mine. The kiss was a slow, deep kiss that I used to express the emotions surging through me.

There was no rush to him, but no hesitation either. Balanced on his elbows, he took his time, savoring being there with me until I was shaking with need beneath him. I shifted, spreading my legs, eager to feel him inside me, but he groaned into my mouth and broke the kiss off.

He rained kisses on my cheeks then growled into my ear, "How many times do you want to come?"

"Me?" I was beyond being able to think straight.

He chuckled and looked down into my eyes. "Yes, you."

I swallowed as I struggled to understand what response he was hoping for. "Sorry, I've never been asked that. What do most women say?"

A shadow darkened his eyes. "I don't want to think about other women, and I don't want to imagine you with anyone but me."

Intense.

Possessive.

So fucking hot. I ran my tongue across my suddenly dry lips. "Three?" I blurted. "Unless that's too much." When he didn't immediately say anything, I added, "You know I've only been with one guy and to be honest it wasn't all that good. I'd be thrilled to even have one."

Anger flashed in his eyes but was quickly replaced by a look I was familiar with—tender concern for me—then amusement. "Three it is—unless you decide you want more. I'm not done until you are, understand?"

I nodded quickly, then joked, "Don't hurt yourself."

His chest rumbled against my breasts as he laughed. "Oh, Katie, a little pain can be fun."

My eyes rounded.

He winked then, without giving me time to overthink what he'd said, began to kiss his way down my neck. From the back of my ear to the spot just below my navel he didn't leave an inch of me unclaimed by those lips of his. Sucking, nipping, teasing until a wave of warmth spread through me—a climax unlike any I'd ever given myself. It was intense, but comforting, like a hug from the inside.

I gripped the bedsheets on either side of me when he worked his magic lower. His breath teased before his fingers spread my sex for his tongue to explore. I didn't like to think of him with anyone else, but when he went to work on my clit with an expertise unlike anything I'd ever imagined, I couldn't resent any of them. Holy shit, no wonder women flocked to his bed.

His fingers plunged deep within me, sliding in and out, stretching me but also seeking a spot that drove me wild when he found it. I bucked against his mouth, crying out, begging him to keep doing whatever the hell he was doing. Years without sex wouldn't have been as easy to endure had I known this was possible.

"So wet," he murmured against my sex. "So perfect."

"Thank you?"

His laugh sent a delicious burst of hot breath across my clit before his tongue began to move more powerfully back and forth, faster and faster across it. There was no reprieve from the pleasure he brought. I widened for him, willing to go wherever he wanted to take me.

And take me he did. My second climax rocked through me like an electrical current, almost too powerful to enjoy and so good tears ran down my cheeks. I gripped his hand, needing a temporary halt of movement as I came floating back from it.

"You like that, baby?"

"Yes," I breathed. I'd never imagined myself as someone who'd like being called baby, but I was feeling so good I wouldn't have protested if he'd tattooed it across my forehead.

"What else do you like?"

Still gasping for air, I admitted, "I don't know." Even as I said the words, something in me changed and that became no longer true. I scooted backward a little and sat up. "I do know what I want."

His hand slid up my leg to cup my sex as he moved upward on the bed as well and propped himself up on one elbow beside me. "And what is that?" As he asked the question, one of his fingers slid between my folds and began to move slowly back and forth across my now sensitive clit.

"I want to be as good as you are at this."

His hand stilled. "For me?"

"Of course." Did he think I saw him as some kind of course I'd take before moving on?

He rolled onto his back, lifting me as he did, then settling me, knees on the sides of his head, and my sex mere inches from his face. Unsure, I remained perfectly still then shuddered when his hands cupped my ass and thrust me downward onto his face.

If his fingers had been magical, his thick, thrusting tongue was sinful. In and out, alternating between my clit and plunging into me. Hot. Wet. Twisting and circling. I leaned forward, balancing myself on the headboard of the bed as he tongue-fucked me so deeply I screamed his name as wave after wave of pleasure shot through me.

I was shaken, sweaty, and weak by the time he moved me off him and reached for a condom. Learning to please him would have to wait until I could lift a limb. He settled himself between my legs then moved them up onto his shoulders and drove that thick cock of his deep inside me with one powerful thrust.

Heaven.

He pounded into me mercilessly. So big he filled me to the point of discomfort, but there was pleasure in that as well. Gone was all the tenderness and patience. This was a primal mating, savage and without restraint. I wasn't sure I would survive, but if there was any way I wanted to go that would have been it.

I expected a quick release from him, but just when I thought he might come, he withdrew and flipped me over onto my knees before him. Sated, but so ready for more, I yelled, "Fuck, yes," when he dug his hand into the back of my hair and yanked my head back as he entered me from behind. The slap of his hand across my butt cheek stung but sent mind-blowing sensations through me.

Relentlessly he thrust in and out, deeper and harder, riding out that orgasm with me until finally grunting and joining me. A moment later, dazed enough that my mouth hung open, I found myself tucked to his side beneath the blanket.

The kiss he gave my forehead nearly had me bursting into tears. *So, that's what sex is supposed to be like.*

Perhaps because I hadn't moved yet on my own accord, he rose onto an elbow and asked, "You okay? I know it's been a while for you. I probably should have—"

I covered his mouth with my hand. "It was perfect."

He smiled against my fingers then relaxed, pulling me back into his arms. "I *may* have spent a lot of time imagining what I wanted to do to you if we ever got together."

I buried my face in his shoulder. "Me too. It wasn't like that with—"

His kiss stopped me there. "I'm not the jealous type. I've never cared about before or after, but when I imagine you with another man . . . especially the one who hurt you . . . I've always regretted not being the one who found you that day. I would have killed him."

His words hit me on so many levels. "I'm glad you didn't because then you wouldn't have been able to sit with me afterward and tell me it wasn't my fault. You'll never know how much your visits that week meant to me. I felt betrayed, but worse—ashamed. I wanted to hide from the world, but you didn't let me. I'd tell you to leave and you'd just sit there anyway, telling me that everything would be okay." I blinked back tears. "You might not have found me that night, but you stopped me from losing myself afterward."

He sighed and hugged me closer. "I'm glad you didn't listen when I told you to leave earlier."

The beat of his heart was steady and strong beneath my ear. "I'm so sorry about your parents."

"Thank you."

I closed my eyes and inhaled him. Levi might tell others he was okay, but he knew I'd call him on that lie. "What happened to them?"

"Boating accident according to Bradford."

"Boating? Where *were* your parents?"

"I didn't ask because I . . . I don't want to know."

"Because wherever they were was somewhere they chose over you?"

His voice was hoarse. "Yes." After a moment, he added, "And they were still together. Was he still drinking and hitting her? I don't want to think about that. It's easier to not ask any questions at all."

I understood that. "That's how I used to feel about my future and what I want to do with it. It was easier to coast along and pretend I was happy as I was. That's not enough anymore."

"You're still set on working with Bradford?"

"Yes and no. I don't really want to engage in shoot-outs, but Joanna has shown me ways I can help the cause without being on the front line." I ran my hand up his muscular biceps. "I heard you were impressive. I know you did the training for me, but what will you do now?"

"I don't know yet. Bradford and I have an understanding. My place is in Driverton, making sure whoever he crosses out there never has a chance to dish out payback here."

Yes, I could see Levi taking that role. He had the heart of a protector.

Yawning, I pulled the blanket higher over both of us.

"Levi?"

"Yes?" he murmured.

"Four. I had four."

He chuckled, stretched to turn off the light then settled back against me. Our breathing deepened in unison. I was dancing on the edge of sleep when he said my name. "Katie?"

"Mmmmm?"

"We're not going back to being friends."

My heart raced with joy. "Good."

A few moments passed before he spoke again. "Katie?"

I answered without opening my eyes. "Yes?"

"Is the steak in the fridge?"

I laughed softly. "Yes. It's marinating."

"Text your aunt and tell her you can't cover the breakfast shift. I intend to have you for breakfast then steak and mac and cheese for lunch."

I smiled into the darkness. "And what do I get?"

He shifted closer and whispered exactly how he'd wake me—where he'd start and how I'd finish. His description included tips on how to drive him wild as well. As I imagined each touch he described, I slid my hand down his stomach and discovered I wasn't the only one his talk was exciting.

Feeling emboldened, I wrapped my hand around his cock and loved how it swelled beneath my touch. "I think I get the idea of what you like, but I'd like to check to make sure."

"I'm all yours."

Forever or for a night, I wasn't sure, but either way I wasn't about to waste a moment of it. I slid beneath the blanket and kissed my way down his stomach. I took him just an inch inside my mouth, just as he'd said he enjoyed, and I swirled my tongue around his tip. When he moaned, I opened my mouth wider and took him deeper.

He dug a hand into my hair. "Oh, fuck, yes."

I wouldn't have thought I'd be ready yet for another round of lovemaking, but pleasing him had me tingling with anticipation. I brought him to the edge of orgasm, then lowered myself onto him and rode him with an abandon I hadn't known myself capable of until we both found glorious release. I collapsed onto his chest. He hugged me to him, and I fell asleep smiling.

Chapter Fourteen

Levi

A S I WOKE the next morning it took me a moment to
realize I wasn't still dreaming, and Katie was actually
naked and cuddled to me—snoring. So damn adorable I
don't know how long I soaked in the sight of her.

We'd done what I told myself could never happen and
somehow the world hadn't ended. A flush ran up my neck
and my cock swelled as memories of how good being with
her had been. Did I think she could do better than me? Yes.
But I was no longer worried I couldn't remain faithful to her.
Whatever this was—it was entirely different than anything
I'd ever experienced. When she'd asked me to stop sleeping
with other women, I'd thought it would be difficult. It
hadn't been.

Staying away from Katie . . . now that had been a hell I'd
only survived by releasing my frustration on Bradford when
we'd sparred. I'd been angry with Ollie for not considering
me good enough for Katie and angry with myself for making

a promise to Ollie I wasn't sure I could keep.

Looks like I'm going to Boston soon. This wasn't the kind of thing I could hide or tell my best friend over the phone. *He'll be angry, but he'll get over it.*

I hope.

I slid my arm out from beneath Katie, trying not to wake her, but her eyes fluttered open. "Hey," I said before giving in to the temptation to kiss her softly.

She smiled against my lips. "Morning."

I could have stayed there, smiling back at her forever. "You snore," I teased.

She brought a hand to her mouth in horror. "I do not." The move sent the covers sliding off her, revealing an even more enticing view.

I cupped one of her breasts and bent my head to kiss the tip of it. "It's adorable, just like the rest of you."

I caught pleasure flashing in her eyes when I raised my gaze to meet hers. She said, "You don't look freaked out that it's morning and I'm still here."

"I'm not."

She shifted to sit up, so I did as well. We stared into each other's eyes for a long moment before she whispered, "No matter how you feel this morning, I don't regret a moment of last night. I want you to know that. I also don't want you to feel pressured to—"

"Stop." Reaching out for her hand, I laced my fingers through hers. "I'm no hero and certainly no saint, but you matter to me. What we did last night matters."

She searched my face. "What comes next?"

I didn't know how to be less than honest with her, so I didn't even try. "I don't know, but together we'll figure it out."

Her fingers tightened on mine. "I like that."

My stomach rumbled, reminding me that I hadn't eaten since lunch the day before. "Go back to sleep for a bit. I'll make breakfast and bring you some."

She smiled and caressed my chest with her free hand. "Breakfast in bed? Are you a romantic?"

"Only with you." I tugged her forward and kissed her deeply. My stomach grumbled again. I groaned, broke off the kiss, and said, "Tempting as you are, I'm hungry as hell. A hangry man is never a good fuck."

"Go eat," she said with a laugh then waved for me to leave. "You set the bar high last night. I didn't tell my aunt I wasn't coming in for nothing." Her mouth rounded. "Oh, shit. I never did text her."

A glance at the clock revealed that it wasn't yet an issue. "I'll find your phone."

"Thanks!" She hopped out of bed, grabbed one of my T-shirts off my chair and pulled it over her head. It covered her almost to her knees and was sexy as hell. I took a step toward her. Food could wait. She said, "Last time I saw my phone was in the back pocket of my jeans."

Her phone. I'd almost forgotten about it. Grabbing a pair of boxer briefs, I headed downstairs. Her phone was easy enough to locate in the pile of clothing we'd discarded hastily onto the floor of my kitchen. I brought it, as well as the rest of our clothing, up to the bedroom then left her to make the call.

I was scrambling eggs in a bowl when Ollie strode in without so much as a knock or warning. *Shit.*

His hands were clenched at his sides and his eyes narrowed as he looked around. "Why is Katie's car in your driveway? Are you fixing it for her?"

I sighed. This wasn't how he should have found out. "We don't have to do this. You already know she's here."

He aggressively stomped forward. "No, I don't. I know some things. I know my best friend would never use news about the death of his parents to fuck my cousin."

Rolling my shoulders back, I fought to remain calm. He had a right to be angry. This was the first promise I'd ever made to him then broken. "I didn't need an excuse."

Well, that came out wrong.

Which could have been why I didn't try to evade his punch. My head snapped back at the blow, but I held my ground.

"What the fuck, Levi?" he growled and swung again.

This time, I ducked but kept my hands at my sides. "What I meant was that I've felt this way about Katie for a long time."

His face went red. "That makes it better? You swore you wouldn't touch her."

I had. In his place, I would have felt betrayed as well.

That didn't change what had happened, though, or that Katie and I were together. "We're not kids. This isn't the kind of thing a pinkie swear can prevent."

Between gritted teeth, he snarled, "Do you at least love her?"

That knocked me back onto my heels more than his punch had. Love? Did I know what that was?

Ollie shoved me back a step. "You could have any woman in the state, hell, you've already done your best to—Why Katie? Why couldn't you keep your dick in your pants and your hands off . . .?"

"Ollie stop," Katie said urgently from the doorway. The sight of her in my shirt did nothing to calm Ollie.

"Katie, go put some clothes on." Ollie said harshly, "This is between me and Levi."

I moved to stand between them. "Ollie, you're my best friend—"

"Not after today," he countered.

I squared my shoulders and went nose-to-nose with him. "That's up to you. If this ends our friendship, so be it. You've been like a brother to me, but I will choose her every single time. *Every single time.* So be very careful before you use that tone with her again."

Katie was beside us, placing a hand on each of our arms. "Levi, could you give me a moment with Ollie?"

That wasn't going to happen, not while Ollie was still furious.

Her hand shook my arm until my attention was pulled to her. There was no fear in her eyes, only determination. "Please," she said quietly.

I held her gaze—my need to protect her warring with my respect for her. He was her family and I'd never seen Ollie raise his hand to a woman. Exhaling audibly, I nodded, but couldn't help but turn to face Ollie one more time. "Before you waste time debating if you can forgive me, ask yourself why you have no faith in my ability to be good to Katie. And if your opinion of me is so low that you can't imagine any outcome other than me hurting her—are you and I even friends? Because I don't think so." I leaned in again and growled, "I'll be right outside the door. Raise your voice to Katie once and your ass will hit the gravel outside so fast your head will spin and you won't be welcome in my home again."

Chapter Fifteen

Katie

*Y*OU'VE BEEN LIKE *a brother to me, but I will choose her every single time. Every single time.*

Those words had ricocheted through me, touching me more deeply than any declaration of love could have. I knew how much Ollie meant to Levi.

Fucking Ollie. Why had he put Levi in the position where he had to choose?

As soon as Levi was out the door, I waved a finger at my cousin. "You're in the wrong here and I love you enough to help you realize it."

Looking at the wall instead of me, he said, "I don't expect you to understand, Katie."

"I understand more than you think I do." I hugged my arms to my stomach. Lately I'd been determined to look ahead and not back, but there were some things that clearly still needed to be resolved—things we didn't talk about because they were too uncomfortable to say out loud. "How you're feeling right now is not Levi's fault. It may feel like it is, but he's not the one you're angry with."

Ollie folded his arms across his chest. "No?"

"You were also affected by what happened to me. It's why you can't let it go. That's what this is about."

Without looking at me, he frowned. "No, this is about Levi and his inability to keep his word."

"Stop punishing Levi because you feel guilty that you weren't the one who found me. Neither one of you could have known how quickly things would go bad. You are a wonderful cousin and he's a good friend."

"Friend," Ollie echoed dryly.

My temper flared. "You're worried if you don't keep me safe, something bad will happen again, but you can't live my life for me. It's time to start trusting me and Levi."

Ollie's silence was a good sign. It meant he didn't disagree.

I continued but lowered my voice so only Ollie could hear, "I have a working theory about us. Staying behind when everyone else left for college stunted us. I've been afraid to want more than I have. Levi still believes anyone who cares about him will leave. You need to find something you're interested in and shift all of these emotions there."

His jaw tensed visibly. "Wow, so glad I came home to make sure Levi was okay."

I took a moment to find the words to express what I was beginning to realize. "Ollie, sometimes when you've loved someone for a long time you form an opinion of them that doesn't allow them room to grow. I'm not the girl who was so desperate to leave Driverton that I was blinded by it. And Levi doesn't need to prove to you that he's good enough for me. You should already know he is."

His stance relaxed slightly. "I just don't want to see you get hurt again—either of you."

"I know. You need to tell him that your reaction is also out of worry for him. He's been a good friend to you. He deserves to know that you're a twisted mash of anxiety and love."

"I wouldn't go that far."

"It's okay to be as long as that's not where you remain. We're on a journey—all three of us. We have an opportunity to do more than sit back and wish we'd made better choices. So, let's give each other the grace to discover who we could be and celebrate our wins instead of holding each other back."

Ollie ran a hand through his hair. "I hate it when you're right."

Deciding it was time to lighten the mood a little, I joked, "The real struggle is being right as often as I am. It's a burden."

He smiled at that.

I added, "I'm going to go put on some underwear and let the two of you talk it out."

Ollie made a face. "I am never walking in here again

without knocking."

"That's probably for the best." I laughed and left the kitchen through the door I knew Levi was outside of. When I saw the tension still in him, I went up onto my tiptoes and kissed him on the cheek. "It's safe to go back."

He ran a thumb over my cheek. "If it wasn't safe, I would never have left you."

"You know what I mean."

His smile was gentle. "I do. You okay?"

I nodded. "You know Ollie, he's all growl but no bite. I don't know how he found out about your parents, but he came home because he was worried about you. His emotions were already high." When Levi didn't say anything, I added, "He's just as worried that I'll hurt you as he is that you'll hurt me."

Shaking his head, Levi asked, "He said that?"

"Go talk to him." I glanced down at the half-cocked package straining against the front of his boxers. "But maybe put pants on first."

Chapter Sixteen

Levi

OLLIE WAS IN the living room by the time I returned. He rose from the couch as I entered the room and said, "Sorry I punched you."

I touched the cheek that was still tender from that hit. "No, you're not."

He flashed a smile. "You're right, you deserved that."

I reluctantly smiled back. "I did."

After clearing his throat, he said, "Everette called when he found out about your parents. We probably have about fifteen minutes before he comes over. He and Shelby had an appointment this morning or they'd already be here."

"Does everyone in town know?"

He shrugged. "Probably. You know how things spread."

I did. Driverton wasn't the place to live if someone wanted privacy. It was only then that I noticed how different Ollie looked. Like me, he'd bulked up. "You've been working out."

He nodded. "Daily. After rehab, I stayed with Clay at his place outside of Boston. I knew Clay was rich, but there is nothing that man doesn't have. His house has a huge gym with an on-call trainer. I thought I'd just be taking a computer course, but Clay suggested a more rounded approach to self-improvement."

"What does that mean?"

"I'm studying finance, sharpshooting, cyber security, and coding. The Barringtons couldn't be kinder. Grant is teaching me how to build generational wealth. Asher is a business deal powerhouse. They call him the hammer and I understand why. He chooses a goal and then doesn't let anything stand in his way. He's allowed me to shadow him, and I understand now that improving my life has to happen here first." He tapped his temple. "Andrew taught me some combat skills and Kade is giving me helicopter lessons. Me. I'm still flat broke, but I feel like I can do anything."

"A helicopter, huh?" He nodded. "*No, shit?* I'm happy for you."

"You look like you've been working out as well." He flexed a bicep then motioned toward mine.

"I've been digging ditches, putting up fencing, and getting my ass kicked by Bradford and his Navy SEAL buddies."

Looking like he was holding back a smile, Ollie said, "So, almost the same thing."

I chuckled at that.

"Did you break your nose while I was gone?" He pointed toward my face.

I touched the still swollen bridge of it. "Possibly. Bradford is a tough bastard."

Ollie held up one of his hands. "I had a callous right there from climbing up the ladder of Clay's yacht too many times the weekend he took me to the Amalfi Coast and rented water obstacle courses."

I barked out a laugh. "You're serious?"

Ollie's grin was shameless. "It's been a pretty good two months." His expression turned more serious. "I haven't touched a drop of alcohol since I left, and I haven't been tempted."

I smiled. "Now that's the news I was hoping to hear."

He inhaled. "Thank you."

"I'm glad it worked out."

After a pause, he said, "I've been an ass about Katie. It's not that I don't think you're good enough for her—"

"I know."

"I also don't want you to get hurt."

"We're good, Ollie. If I could have, I would have kept that promise. It was just that—"

"You don't have to explain. In fact, I can guarantee it'll be better if you don't." He cleared his throat. "I'm grateful for everything you've been doing for me. When I start making money, I'll slide you some for helping out at Little Willie's."

"So, you also want a broken nose."

His eyebrows rose. "No. No, I don't. But I do know you've been working there daily for no compensation and that's a bigger favor than anyone should ask a friend for."

I looked him over for the first time, taking in the upgrade to his attire. Gone was the T-shirt and jeans. In its place was a polo shirt and trousers. Hiking boots? Replaced by leather shoes. "I get the feeling you'll be going back to Boston."

"I will be—for now. It's not about the money, it's about finding out what I'm capable of, and I can't do that here. I've considered closing Little Willie's until I know what I'm doing."

"Don't. People need a place to gather. We'll keep it going until you decide what you want to do."

"I can't ask you to do that. It's my burden to bear."

"You didn't. Working there is important to Katie. It wouldn't be fair if you took that from her while you go off and find yourself. She doesn't see it as a burden."

"No, she doesn't." He blinked a few times quickly as if he hadn't considered her attachment to it. He tucked his hands in the pockets of his trousers. "I'll leave it open, then. If you're sure . . ."

I nodded once.

Ollie's shoulder rose then fell as he accepted the situation. "Nothing in Boston was more important than being here when I heard about your parents."

"Thank you."

"Is it true that you have no interest in where they were?"

"It doesn't matter."

"It might."

"They're still dead either way."

"Yes, but you need closure."

"Now you sound like a therapist."

"I've talked to a couple recently and I'm glad I did. I had shit I needed to work out before I could see myself as someone who deserved success. You have a few things you might have to face before you can as well."

"I'm fine the way I am."

"Friend to friend, you're not. If you really do want to be with Katie, figure yourself out. Stop settling for surviving. She deserves the man I know you can be."

"I liked you better when you were punching me in the face."

"I can do that again if you think it'll help."

"This time I'd hit back."

Fully dressed, Katie walked into the room. "There's no blood on the rug, so can I assume you've worked things out?"

"For now," Ollie said.

Tentatively, as if testing the waters, Katie came to my side. I put an arm around her waist and looked Ollie in the eye. Our friendship was important to me, but it would crumble if he didn't respect Katie's decision to be with me.

He looked from me to her and back, and I tensed as I waited for his reaction. Katie peered up at me with both concern and determination. My arm tightened around her in support. I wanted to tell her everything was fine, but I wasn't yet convinced it was.

"I'll give you six months to propose then a year to marry," Ollie said in a low tone. "More than that, and I'm no longer okay with this." He pinned me with an intensity I wasn't used to from him. "And to be clear, you cheat on her, and I'll bury you alive in the field behind my mother's house."

"A year, so generous." Katie and I exchanged an amused look. That was as close to hearing Ollie say he approved of us together as we'd probably ever get. She joked, "But buried alive? That's hardcore."

"I'd do the same to anyone who hurt you, so I accept the terms."

Smiling, she gasped and brought a hand to her chest. "You'd bury someone alive for me? Never let it be said that the men of Driverton aren't romantic."

We all shared a laugh even though neither Ollie nor I had been joking.

"I was making breakfast," I said. "Ollie, you're welcome to join us. I'll make extra in case Everette and Shelby drop by."

"I should probably go," he said grudgingly. "But I *am* hungry."

Katie motioned toward the kitchen. "I have everything to make my steak and mac and cheese. We could cook both and call it brunch."

One of Ollie's eyebrows raised in question. "Your homemade mac and cheese? Well, now I can't leave."

"Oh, good," I said under my breath.

Katie pinched my side lightly. "Great. This is good. It'll give us all a chance to catch up."

She correctly interpreted my smirk. Brunch with our friends wasn't how I'd imagined the morning going. Still, these were our best friends. Any attempt to conceal that things had changed between Katie and me would be a waste of time. They'd know the first time they saw us together. "Brunch it is."

We'd hardly been in the kitchen any time at all when Everette and Shelby appeared at the door. It was normal for my friends to come and go without knocking. I'd always considered my home theirs as well and, as a rule, hadn't brought dates there.

I might need to talk to them about that.

Everette came right over to me and gave me a bear hug that practically lifted me off my feet. "Sorry I couldn't be here earlier."

When the heels of my feet touched the ground, I smiled and pushed him off me. "I'm fine."

He was a big oaf, but one of the nicest people I'd ever known. Whoever had coined the term "heart of gold" must have had him in mind. Not only was he often the first person to offer to help someone in need, but he genuinely liked nearly everyone. It was something that had gotten him in trouble a time or two, but no situations Ollie and I hadn't been able to extricate him from. He was also the perfect fit for Shelby. She'd been through some stuff and had lost faith in humanity. If anyone was able to bring that side of someone back, it was Everette. I'd never steal from anyone, but I swear if he ever caught me taking money from his wallet, he'd be more concerned about what I needed it for than the betrayal itself. He was one of those who saw good in people even when there wasn't any.

As he stood there with his big, goofy smile, looking like he wanted to hug me again, I was reminded of how different Bradford was with him. Understandable, I guess. It's hard to punch someone who looks so eager to please.

"Are you guys hungry?" Katie asked. "We were just about to cook up steak, eggs, and mac and cheese."

Everette looked from Katie to me and back. I nodded once. He smiled then turned to assess Ollie's reaction. When Ollie rolled his eyes and shrugged, Everette's face lit up.

With a shake of her head, Shelby asked, "What did I miss?"

Katie's gaze met mine, looking so uncertain I stepped closer to her and took her hand in mine. Her smile must have been mirrored on my face because Everette gurgled with humor, which gained him a grunt from Ollie. I countered with a groan.

Katie winked at Shelby. "It's a primitive language, but I can translate for you."

Shelby laughed. "I'd love that, thanks."

Katie held up our interlaced hands. "Levi and I are," she met and held my gaze before adding, "taking our friendship to the next level. Ollie worries about me, so this is hitting him hard and that amuses the shit out of Everette."

"Oh, that's awesome." Shelby's smile was sincere. "And about time from what Everette has told me. How incredible to have known each other your whole lives and then take that leap."

Katie let out a shaky breath. "It *is* a leap."

I brought her hand to my mouth and kissed it. "But we're taking it together."

She smiled up at me from beneath her lashes. "Yes, we are."

"So, who's making the eggs?" Ollie asked, and there was a collective laugh.

"Why don't you start them?" I suggested. I'd never been a romantic man or one who was into public displays of affection, but it was impossible to look away from Katie when she smiled at me that way.

"You're going to get your ass kicked," Katie said impishly.

"He can try, but I have a feeling his training wasn't as intense as mine. I can still take him," I joked.

Ollie mumbled something that both Katie and I ignored.

There were some moments a person didn't want to end, and that was one I knew I'd remember for the rest of my life. Katie had just announced to our friends that we were together and nothing had ever felt so right.

Chapter Seventeen

Katie

HOURS LATER, I was standing on the porch, leaning back against Levi, wrapped in the comfort of his arms as our friends drove away. Brunch together had gone so well that Everette suggested we make it a regular thing. My breath still caught in my throat when I imagined that this could be my life.

Levi nuzzled my neck. I closed my eyes and savored the feel of him around me. What had seemed like an impossibility no longer did. Levi and I were . . . together.

And it wasn't a secret.

Not that it would have been for long, anyway. My aunt had known the moment I'd told her I wasn't able to cover the breakfast shift. I didn't even consider lying because only a fool would lie in a town as small as Driverton. Our definition of a secret was any topic we'd collectively decided to not talk about after everyone in town had talked about it. That was likely the reason Levi had wanted to ensure that Ollie returned more than just sober—because even if we never said a word, people would know where he'd been. And he'd know they knew.

Not everyone would be as easy as Everette and Shelby were to win over. Did I dare hope my parents and brother would handle the news well?

"What are you thinking?" Levi murmured against my ear.

I relaxed into his embrace. "Nothing important."

He hugged me closer and tucked my head beneath his chin. "You know how you can always tell when I'm lying?"

"Yes."

"I can tell when your thoughts start racing. What are you worried about?"

Rather than feeling exposed, I felt seen. I thought back to all the times he'd stepped in to help me when no one else had noticed I was in need. "Aunt Reana knows I'm here."

"Okay."

"And Ollie and Everette."

He made a sound deep in his chest. "You're worried about how your parents will react."

"And my brother. Tom can be overprotective like Ollie at times. I should have called home last night to tell them I was sleeping out. Since they didn't call me . . ."

"You think they already know?"

I grimaced into the bright afternoon sun. "There's a good chance they do."

"Do they have a problem with me?"

I wanted to spare him from the truth, but I wasn't willing to lie to him. He knew his reputation and what my parents thought of his bed-hopping.

He inhaled deeply, his chest expanding against my back. "Katie, I can't go back and be anyone but who I've been, and I don't regret any of it."

"I'm not suggesting that you should. They'll just believe that's who you'll be with me."

Turning me in his arms, he raised my face until I was forced to meet his gaze. "All that matters to me is what you believe."

My answer wasn't immediate because I had to search within me for the answer. "I know you'd never hurt me."

"But?"

"When Ollie asked you if you loved me . . ."

He tensed beneath my touch. "If you need me to say the words, I will but . . ."

"But you wouldn't mean them. Then, no, don't say them." I would have been lying if I'd said I wasn't disappointed.

Bending so his forehead rested on mine, he said, "I haven't been with anyone since you asked me not to be, and it wasn't difficult. The idea of you with anyone but me guts me. Is that love?"

I'd asked myself that same question. It was then I saw the real beauty of a strong friendship being the foundation of our relationship. He wasn't feeding me lines or love-bombing me. This was real and his honesty meant more than flattery and flowers ever could.

"I don't know." I smiled. "But I think I'm okay starting there."

"You *think*?" His hands went to my sides and tickled me.

Squirming, I laughed. "Okay, I am."

He tickled me again. "And just *okay*?"

This time, even as I laughed, I pulled back then threw myself upward, trusting him to catch me. He did. I wrapped my legs around his waist and my arms around his neck. "Do you know that in some cultures tickling is considered a form of torture?"

Settling me against him, he opened the door with a free hand and carried me back inside. "Really, which one?"

My grin was shameless. *"Mine."*

He turned and locked the door. "Torture is not what's on the menu for today."

"There's a menu? What's on it?"

"Anything and everything you want." With me clinging to him, he made his way up the stairs to his bedroom.

LATER THAT EVENING, Levi was adamant about making sure I made it home okay. He followed my car, which would have felt awkward had we not talked on the phone the whole way. After weeks of not speaking much, we had a lot to catch up on.

My parents were on the porch as soon as we pulled up the driveway. "Do you want to say hello?" I asked.

"Of course I do."

Of course he does.

I was still unbuckling my seatbelt when he opened my car door. He offered me his hand and I took it. I searched his face. Not releasing my hand after closing the door behind me was a bold move that would send a clear message to my parents. Was he ready for that?

"I am," he answered, and I winced, realizing I'd asked the question aloud. "Are *you*?"

I took a deep breath. "My parents can be a little—"

"Katie, I know them."

"They mean well, but their idea of helpful advice can sting."

"It'll be fine, Katie." He bent his head closer to mine and looked me in the eye. "I have thick skin."

"I don't like to argue with them, but if they say anything about you . . ."

His eyes darkened with emotion. "Never side with me over your family."

Something he'd said to Ollie came back to me. I tightened my fingers around his and said, "Don't tell me what to do. I'll choose you *every time* if I want to."

His grin started in his eyes and then stretched those beautiful lips of his. "What am I going to do with you?"

"After last night and today I have a few ideas for what I'd like to try again."

His laughter released the tension from both of us. "Well, okay, then. I'm ready whenever you are."

It was tempting to say, "Right now" and hop into his car, but if I wanted my parents to accept him, that wouldn't be the best way to win them over. "Okay, let's do this."

I didn't have to explain that I meant to face my parents. He knew me well.

My parents' expressions were difficult to discern as we approached the porch. Still holding hands, we stopped at the bottom of the steps. I spoke first, "Sorry I didn't call."

My mother's lips pursed.

My father straightened and waited.

The door behind them opened, and my brother, still dressed in his sheriff uniform, stepped out onto the porch beside them. My voice croaked as I said, "Hi, Tom. I didn't see your car."

"It's out back." His stance mirrored my father's.

Levi frowned then gave my hand a squeeze. "Always good to see you, Tom."

My brother made a sound that reminded me so much of Ollie I almost laughed but didn't think any of them would share my amusement. Instead, I forced a bright smile and said, "I'm glad you're all here. Levi and I have something we want to tell you."

My mother gasped, "You're pregnant."

"No." It was my turn to frown. I loved my mother, but she went from zero to a hundred way too often. "Why would you say that?"

She threw her hands up. "It was a wild guess, but that's the best I have since you don't tell me anything lately."

"You said there wasn't a single thing I was doing that you approved of. That's kind of a conversation killer."

Tom put his arm around her—*the suck-up.* "Katie, is that really fair?"

It wasn't, but I glared at him anyway then sighed. "Between working at Little Willie's and training with Joanna and Bradford, I know I haven't been around much, but things have been going really well." I paused and smiled at Levi. "Really well."

My father sighed and opened the door. "Come on in, you two. Whatever you have to tell us, I have a feeling I should have a beer when I hear it."

Walking in the house before him, my mother said loudly, "I don't even drink, but get me one as well, please."

Tom met us at the top of the stairs. He opened his mouth to say something but before he was able to get a word out, I held up a finger between us and said, "This is important to me, Tom."

As young siblings, Tom and I had driven each other crazy, especially when it came to teasing each other. It was our mother who'd taught us to be clear with each other when something crossed a line or was important.

Tom looked from me to Levi. "It's not like we didn't all see this coming, but Levi . . ."

Levi nodded.

Tom continued, "I like you. Don't make me lose my pension over something stupid like giving you a beatdown."

After training with Bradford that was not the threat it might have been months earlier, but Levi kindly didn't mention that. He said, "I don't intend to give you a reason to."

"Good," Tom said. "How did Ollie take the news?"

Levi exhaled a whistle. "About as good as expected, but he's okay with it now."

"I'm glad," Tom said quietly. "And I was sorry to hear about your parents." The look he gave Levi was so sweet I left Levi's side to hug him.

"Thank you," Levi said.

After I returned to Levi's side, Tom said, "Congratulations. I heard you aced every test Bradford threw at you."

"I did okay."

"Much better than okay. He tried to break you, and when he couldn't, you earned his admiration. I don't hear Bradford talk up many people, but he has only good things to say about you."

"That means a lot to me. Thanks."

Watching the two of them together I was bursting with pride. Yes, the men in my life could be stubborn and over-protective, but beneath their bristles, they were good, kind people. My parents would come around to the idea of Levi and me.

They'd have to.

"Are we good now?" I asked. "Can we go inside?"

Tom nodded then said, "We're good." And held out a hand to Levi.

They shook hands then smiled at each other like they'd just become best friends. I walked into the house before them, hopeful that everyone else would come around as quickly.

Chapter Eighteen

Levi

TOM LED US into the house. The Berbers were already in the living room. Standing in front of one of the couches, Katie's father took a swig of beer as soon as we joined them. Her mother held an unopened beer so tightly I wondered if she might crush it. Tom offered to get me a drink. I declined. The day might come when I could have one without having ten, but for now, it was easier to not indulge in any.

We stood in painful silence for long enough that I glanced at Katie to assess how she was faring. She looked poised to go to battle for me and that saddened me. The Berbers were a good family. Yes, her parents held strong opinions on what they wanted for their daughter, but it was only because they wanted to see her happy and able to support herself.

All Katie wanted was the same.

The closed expressions on Katie's parents' faces might once have had me on the defense. It didn't that day. I knew my reputation with women. Hell, I'd earned it. Their concern for Katie when it came to me didn't offend me or make me think less of them. In fact, I would have been disappointed in them if they weren't concerned. Knowing my history, I wouldn't want someone like me to date a daughter of mine.

My past paled in importance in the face of my future. Bradford had helped me see that. I cleared my throat and said, "We're not strangers, which means you've seen me at my best and my worst over the years . . ."

Katie's grip on my hand tightened. "You don't have to explain yourself."

I gave her temple a quick kiss. "I want to."

"Go on," her father said.

"I'm aware of what you're worried about. I would be too if I were you. I was a heavy drinker, avoided responsibility and relationships, and didn't have a single goal until recently."

"You're not selling yourself well, son," her father said, but there was a gentle humor to his tone.

Her mother sighed and shook her head.

I continued, "But I've learned a few things over the past few months that changed the way I live my life. The first was to stop trying to change the past. It's done and gone. There's not a thing that can be done about it. It's like trying to go for a walk backward. You can put energy into it, but if your focus is on what's behind you, all you'll do is keep falling on your ass."

"That's actually good advice," her mother said.

"I'll tell Bradford you approve. Just so you know, he reminds me of you."

"Me?" Her eyes rounded and she appeared slightly offended.

"He takes no nonsense, but genuinely wants the best for all those around him."

Surprise then pleasure lit her eyes. "I do have a low threshold for bullshit."

I nodded, "I've always liked that about your family. Katie has a lot of you in her." That gained me a wide-eyed look from Katie, but I wasn't saying anything that wasn't true, so I continued. "For as long as I can remember, Katie has been there reminding Ollie, Everette, Cooper, and me to do better—be kinder to each other—try harder. We grumble at her, but only because when she calls us out she's so right it hurts."

Katie smiled sheepishly. "I didn't realize I did that."

Pulling her to my side, I said, "It's not something you should ever change. You've been a lighthouse beacon, guiding us when stupidity fogged our brains."

She beamed a smile at me. "There were some pretty foggy years."

Tearing my attention from her beautiful face, I looked her father in the eye. "She's the reason we agreed to work with Bradford, and I can't begin to explain how much of an impact that has had on our lives."

He nodded in approval.

Her mother interjected, "I do see all of your lives chang-ing, but are you sure it's for the better? If he doesn't intend to bring a dangerous element to Driverton, why does he have everyone training like they're going into battle?"

Katie was the one who answered her. "It's all he knows. He's a survivor and someone who can't sit back and do nothing when someone is in danger. Just like you can't. Just like Dad can't. You know how Dad has to understand fire to be able to put it out? Bradford teaches a person how to face their weaknesses and conquer them so they can stand up for those who can't protect themselves. There's no condition requiring any of us to continue to work with him, but I want to because, through training with him, I've learned about myself and my strengths. I'm no longer afraid to reach for my dreams. I know I'm capable of so much more than I've done to this point."

Her mother's hand went to her mouth and tears filled her eyes. "I may owe Bradford an apology."

I said, "I did. I didn't see the value of what he was offer-ing until I gave it a real chance."

Katie hugged me while looking at her parents. "Levi agreed to work with him only because he wanted to make sure I wasn't just safe—but that I succeeded."

Her mother's demeanor warmed toward me. "Is that true?"

"Yes, ma'am, it is."

Tom went to stand beside his mother again. "As someone who has spent a significant amount of time with the people who came to Driverton via an association with Cooper, I can understand Mom and Dad's concerns, but I also believe the good they bring outweighs the risk."

Katie's parents exchanged a long look then seemed to come to an agreement. Her mother walked toward us and said, "I'm always going to worry about you, but don't ever feel like you can't tell me what you're up to."

Nodding, Katie smiled at her mother then at me. "That seems like the perfect opening to tell you that Levi and I are dating."

In a dry tone, her father said, "Raise your hand if that's news to you."

His wife gave him a light smack to the side. "Daniel Arthur Berber, this is a big moment for Katie. She's never brought a man home to us before."

Tom joked, "Levi has been here a million times if he's been here once."

Katie's mother gave her son a pointed look. "This is different."

I smiled because it was.

Looking suddenly serious, her father asked, "How long has this been going on?"

The emotion in Katie's eyes when she looked at me stole my ability to answer. She spoke instead. "The dating part is recent. The friendship it's based on? I don't remember a time when I didn't enjoy being with Levi."

"Ditto," I said with a smile because I couldn't produce a more coherent response while she was looking at me like I was someone she could spend eternity with.

"Well then, make sure you treat him right," her mother said.

For a moment no one said anything. I wondered, if like I had, they'd all expected her to lecture *me* on how to behave. That she'd chosen to advise Katie on how to treat me was both adorable and hilarious. I couldn't help but laugh at the shocked look on Katie's face.

Thankfully when our eyes met, she started to laugh as well.

Tom joined in, then Daniel, then, reluctantly, Katie's mother. When our laughter subsided, she threw her hands up in the air and said, "I don't know what you all find so amusing—I've always liked Levi."

No one dared laugh at that claim, but I suspect they all wanted to.

Chapter Nineteen

Katie

WHEN MY MOTHER suggested we head out to the backyard, I was sure I wasn't the only one grateful for the fresh air and distraction. My father didn't waste the opportunity of having two strong men available to help with some chores he'd been putting off. They added an extension to his woodshed then started splitting logs to fill it. My mother and I supervised for a bit then went inside to prep for dinner.

While washing some vegetables, my attention was drawn out the kitchen window to where Levi glistened with sweat. The way he raised the ax above his head, muscles rippling up his back, arms flexing, before he brought it down with such power. As someone who had intimate knowledge of how good he was at using all that strength in other ways, I found it impossible to look away.

From beside me, my mother said, "I'm sorry I made you feel like you couldn't talk to me."

"It's okay," I said absently. God, Levi was male perfection. Strong. Protective. Supportive. I really didn't want to sleep above the garage that night.

"I've decided your father has to live in the basement."

"That's nice."

My mother's chuckle drew some of my attention back to her. "I won't bother asking how you feel about him, you're drooling on the carrots."

Reluctantly I turned away from the window and met her gaze. "I never expected to feel this way about him. Now I can't imagine feeling any other way."

She nodded and folded a dishtowel. "I can't believe I'm saying this, but I wholeheartedly approve. He's always cared for you, but I didn't see him as emotionally mature enough for more than that. I liked everything he said earlier. He's done a lot of growing up—and so have you. I'm proud of both of you."

I blinked back emotion and sniffed. "You just want me to hug you with these wet hands of mine."

"Wet is better than sticky, but I've never turned down those either."

I hugged her tightly. When I stepped back, I said, "I'm sorry I get so impatient when you're trying to help me. I may not look like I'm listening to your advice, but apparently, I can't help but go off and share it with others."

She pursed her lips. "We're all a mix of the best and worst of our parents. My parents had strong opinions about a lot of things and some I didn't agree with, which is why I found it so easy to move away from them. I don't ever want us to get to that place. If you ever feel like there's a divide building between us—talk to me. I may not know what to say, but I love you enough to work with you until we get it right."

If she really meant it, there was something I needed to say. "What I really want, more than anything else, is for you to trust me as I flap my wings and learn to fly. I'm going to make some mistakes, but I'm not afraid anymore. And I'm not ashamed."

"You have no reason to be ashamed."

I shrugged. "That doesn't change that it was something I chose to carry the weight of. But I've put it down and moved on. Levi is doing the same with his past. That's why I really think we can make it."

"What will Levi do about his parents?"

"Nothing. He's closed that door."

"He might have to open it—just a crack. Adulting isn't fun and often involves facing things a person doesn't want to. He'll need to know if his parents left his house to him or to someone else."

I gasped. "Could they have done that? Not left it to him?"

"They could if they had a will." She took my hand. "You don't want Levi to think the house is his only to have the new owners swoop in and take it from him. If he really does listen to you, you should advise him to find out what his parents did with their estate."

"You're right."

"Could you say that again? Few words fall better on a mother's ears."

I laughed and rolled my eyes. "I love you, Mom."

"I love you too, sweetie."

Turning so I could see Levi again; I soaked in the perfection of him then wrinkled my nose. "It wouldn't matter to me if he loses the house, and we have to start from scratch. You should have seen him when Ollie looked like he might quit working with Bradford for the second time. Levi was right there making sure that wouldn't cost me my opportunity. He'd walk through hell for me without complaint and take my side in any fight without needing to first determine if I'm right."

"Then he's a keeper."

"I really think he might be."

My mother came to my side and put an arm around me, watching her man giving my man advice even though Levi seemed perfectly capable. "You know, when your father and I started out, we didn't know what we were doing, and we were both broke. None of that mattered in the long run. You'll be fine."

I sniffed and nodded. "I know I will be. I have incredible parents who showed me that I couldn't settle for less than."

"He sure is good looking."

"Mom, keep your eyes on your man."

She chuckled. "What makes you think I wasn't?"

"You got me there." After a pause, I said, "Mom, I probably won't be sleeping here tonight."

"I know *I* wouldn't be," she said with amusement.

I pushed her shoulder playfully. "Stop."

"Sorry, should I pretend to be shocked? You look like you just rolled out of his bed."

My cheeks warmed. "I hoped we were less obvious than that."

"I'd tell you to take things slowly, but your father and I were like a match to kindling. We couldn't keep our hands off each other. When I think of all the places we—"

"Okay, we've bonded enough on that subject for tonight, Mom. What do you say we go back to discussing anything else?"

She laughed. "Did I raise a prude? All I'm saying is enjoy this stage. Sex changes over the life of a relationship. It's still good thirty years in and cycles through periods of being mind-blowing, but there's just something extra special about doing everything for the first time."

"La la la, I can't hear you."

"Just know that if you ever have any questions or want to talk, I'm here."

I didn't want to be in this conversation, but I felt I had to say, "Still mind-blowing even after thirty years? Damn, Mom. That's impressive."

She fluttered her eyelashes at me. "Wait till you see how much your father smiles after you move out."

I gave her a curious look. Living over the garage seemed like it would have given them enough privacy.

She shrugged one shoulder. "How many times a day do you walk in without warning?"

"Oh." My mouth remained round as I saw that from their point of view instead of mine. I didn't have a full kitchen or storage for things like paper towels or cleaning supplies. I was in and out of the main house frequently, sometimes at all hours of the day and night. I'd never imagined that might affect them. "Oh. I'll start knocking."

"Or send a text so we have a heads-up."

"I will." A huge smile spread across my face. "Whether it's with Levi or someone else, I hope I end up married to someone I love so much that I have to ask my adult children to text first."

"You will, sweetie. And if my mother's intuition is right, you've already found him."

Chapter Twenty

Levi

I WOKE WITH a start in the middle of the night and reached for Katie. Without waking, she closed the distance between us and snuggled to my side. As I held her, I let fragments of the nightmare I'd woken from re-enter my thoughts.

For a moment, I was downstairs in the basement of my house with Katie. She was once again asking me, "Where do you see yourself in the future? What brings you joy?"

This time I told her she did, but it wasn't enough. She didn't like any of my responses. She wanted to be with me, but not me as I was.

And just to torture myself, I dreamed myself back in time, only this time it wasn't Mary's mother I proposed to while stoned, it was Katie's.

As I lay there with Katie in my arms, I wondered what it meant—if it meant anything at all. My dreams should have been about reliving the wins of the day. I'd done the seemingly impossible and convinced Ollie and Katie's parents that I was good enough for her.

One stupid dream had me questioning if I was. I could be faithful to her. That wasn't my concern. Other women had lost all appeal. But what kind of future could I promise Katie?

I'd told Bradford that money wasn't important to me, but it might have to be. Katie wanted all the things her parents had: the house, the kids, the security that comes from having a partner who has his shit together. I owned almost nothing, had very little in the bank, and had turned down two jobs that would have made changing that situation possible.

"Are you awake?" Katie asked in a whisper.

I whispered back, "Unfortunately, yes. Go back to sleep."

"I can't. There's something on my mind that's bugging me. I have to say it."

That didn't sound good. I wondered if we'd had the same dream. "You can tell me anything, you know that."

"My mother brought up something today while we were there. I didn't want to ruin the mood earlier by sharing it with you, but I do think it's an important conversation to have."

I braced for the worst. Had her mother brought up something that had made her see a future with me wasn't possible? Was this where she told me she figured out what the difference was between loving someone and being in love with them and what we had was only friendship? "What did your mother think we should discuss?"

She placed a hand on my chest. "Your decision to not know more about what happened to your parents. She thinks you need to know what they did with their estate—with this house. I know it's difficult to think that they may not have left it to you, but if we don't live here, we'll find somewhere else. My parents didn't have anything when they started out and they did fine. Together we'll figure this out."

Together. I rolled her beneath me and dug my hands into her hair. "Every time I think you can't be more incredible; you prove me wrong."

Her relieved sigh warmed my lips. "You're not upset that I agree with her?"

"How could I be when you're both right? I do need to know." Her promise to stay with me even if I had nothing touched a part of me I'd closed off a long time ago. It was easy to imagine people leaving me. I knew how to survive that. It was terrifying to trust that someone would stay—hell or high water. If anyone would, it was Katie.

"So, you'll talk to Bradford about them?"

"First thing tomorrow."

"Do you want me to go with you?"

My knee-jerk reaction was to say, "No, I can do it alone." And I almost said those words, but then I looked into her eyes and saw her love for me. With anyone else, my priority would have been to keep a part of myself closed off, but this was Katie. When it came to her, there were no walls. "I would love that."

She bounced beneath me and smiled. "You would?"

I kissed her lips gently and murmured, "I would." Then I growled, "You know what else I would love?"

Chapter Twenty-One

Katie

W ITH OLLIE BACK in town and temporarily covering all the shifts, Levi and I were free to head over to Bradford's early. We helped Joanna with some of her barn chores because what day could go badly if it started with petting rescue mini horses?

When we finished, we all headed to the main house to wash up and have a quick snack. It was a relaxed morning, but there was also an air of anticipation. Or maybe it was only me who needed Levi to hear something good about his parents.

I knew that ignoring a situation didn't make it go away. It was better to find out the details about the house now rather than be surprised by them later. That didn't make it easier when it came to having the actual conversation. Levi was playing it off like he didn't care one way or the other, but I knew he did. If his parents had left him nothing, or worse, already sold the house out from under him, it would be a final, painful betrayal from the grave.

Gathered in the kitchen, each of us nursing a glass of water, Joanna said, "I heard Ollie's temporarily back. Does that mean the two of you will have a few days off?"

"It does," I said happily.

"Any plans?" she asked.

Levi and I shared a quick but sexually charged look before both looking away. Had we not felt it was important to get some answers for Levi we'd probably both still be running around his house naked.

Bradford coughed on a laugh.

Joanna smiled in approval.

I moved to stand closer to where Levi was leaning against one of the counters. There was no reason to hide anything from Joanna and Bradford. Of all of our friends, they were the most supportive when it came to us dating. Levi looped his arms around my waist and pulled me back to rest against his chest then cleared his throat. "Bradford, I've been meaning to ask you a question."

"Sure," Bradford said.

I hated the wave of tension I felt pass through Levi. *Please let this go well for him. Let him hear something good.*

"It's about my parents. I know I said I didn't care to know anything about where they went or what happened to them, but I've changed my mind."

"Oh," Joanna said.

"What do you want to know?" Bradford asked.

I placed my arms over Levi's, hoping he could feel my

support. He laced the fingers of one of his hands with one of mine. "I'm not even sure. Anything. Everything. Where did they go? Did my father ever stop drinking? Was my mother happy she went with him?"

Bradford sighed. "I can't speak to the last part, but my understanding is that your parents went to Hartford, Connecticut first. Your father has a DUI from that time but nothing about domestic abuse. He and your mother were evicted from their housing after about a year. They slowly made their way down the East Coast, taking short-term jobs, moving on each time your father lost a job and they fell behind on rent."

"Sounds about right," Levi muttered. It was only because I was pressed against Levi that I could feel how much this conversation was affecting him. The muscles in his arms shook with light spasms.

"Did things ever get better for them?" The question was wrung from me.

"I'm not optimistic when it comes to people's ability to change, but when they were living in Georgia, they got into a serious car accident that put them both in the hospital. That must have been a wakeup call for them. After that, both of your parents took live-in jobs at an island resort off the coast of Florida. If their job reviews are anything to go by, things turned around for them."

"That's a lot more detail than I thought you'd have." Levi's voice was tight. "How did you find out they were dead?"

Bradford wasn't one to hesitate, so when he paused before speaking, both Levi and I tensed. Finally, he said, "I've known where they were for a couple of months and made sure I'd be contacted if there were ever a change in their situation."

Levi stilled behind me. "You've known where my parents were for *months*?"

"I have."

"And said nothing?"

Although Bradford didn't look comfortable with the conversation, he held Levi's gaze. "You had no interest in locating them."

"Then why did *you*?"

"I didn't. However, when information regarding their location was presented to me, I brought the option of disclosing those details to you. You were clear about what you wanted in regards to your parents."

I could feel the waves of emotion crashing through Levi. He inhaled sharply then released a long, slow breath. "You are correct. I remember that conversation."

It wasn't as clear-cut to me. "Bradford, I don't know what that conversation entailed, but I can guarantee you left out the key point that you knew where they were."

"I did." Bradford's expression was tight. "That was a mistake."

Joanna slipped under his arm and hugged him. "One that anyone might have made."

Bradford hugged her to his side and seemed to choose his next words with care. "Levi, I based my decision on what my experience has been. I have no relationship with my father and no desire to. If you offered to tell me where he is, I'd tell you I don't care to have that information, but having seen your reaction to the death of your parents, I may need to rethink my expectation that I'll feel nothing when I receive news that he's gone."

His words were so raw and real none of us spoke at first. Bradford's pain was as tangible in that moment as Levi's. I wanted to tell them both they were remarkable men, especially in the face of what they'd survived, but those words didn't feel adequate.

Joanna appeared equally at a loss for what to say.

Levi slowly relaxed behind me. "It's not as simple as caring or not caring. I don't know what I would have said had you told me you knew where my parents were." After a moment, he asked, "You said they died in a boating accident. What happened? I don't remember my parents ever going near water."

"That might explain why they both drowned. According to the police report, your mother fell overboard, and your father jumped in to save her, but ended up drowning with her."

I hoped hearing that brought Levi some comfort. In the end, his father's final act had been selfless and hopefully out of love. "There were witnesses?"

"They were ferrying guests from the mainland to the resort when it happened, so there were several."

In a hoarse voice, Levi asked, "When?"

"A few days ago."

"How did you find out?"

"Their lawyer contacted me."

"Their *lawyer?* Criminal lawyer?"

"No, estate, acting as their trustee. They had all of their assets put into a trust so there would be no dispute if anything happened to them."

"My parents didn't have *assets*," he growled. "Except the house I live in. Are you saying it belongs to a trust?"

"Until you determine if you're the beneficiary, yes."

"Great. That's great. Looks like it'll cost me money to go find out that my parents left me nothing."

I turned in Levi's arms and met his gaze. "You don't know that."

"Why else would they go to the trouble of hiring a lawyer and putting the house in a trust? They wanted to make it harder for me to fight to retain it. I wonder what poor sucker they promised it to and what they exchanged it for."

Bradford shared a look with Joanna. "I don't know if they left the house to you or not, but I do know they had acquired an asset large enough that putting it in a trust made sense."

Levi frowned. "What asset?"

Joanna answered in a cheerful voice. "The island resort

they'd been working at. Apparently they made such a good impression on the elderly owner of it that he left it to them in his will."

"Oh, my God, my parents swindled an old man out of his property?"

"That's one way to look at it, I guess," Bradford said. "Or he had no one else to leave it to and felt they would carry on his vision."

That caught my attention. I bounced with excitement. "What kind of resort is it? Like a sanctuary for rare birds? Is it one of those green, zero-energy consumption places?"

"Not exactly," Bradford said.

I gasped as ideas came to me. "It's a retreat for artists? Or corporate team building? Yoga. It's a resort dedicated to meditation and relaxation."

"It's a nudist resort," Joanna said in a soft voice.

"It's a what?" Levi demanded.

"You heard her," Bradford answered.

"What the hell is a nudist resort?" We all gave him a look that essentially said we understood why he was struggling with the idea, but he didn't need us to explain it. He looked from Bradford to Joanna and back. "You're fucking with me."

They both shook their heads.

"Wow," I said. "I didn't see that one coming."

"So, you may be the new owner of both your house as well as a private island resort," Joanna said with a smile.

"Even if what you're saying is true and they somehow got their hands on any kind of resort, I don't believe they would have left it to me. So, bizarre as that twist of events was for them, it doesn't affect me. All I want to know is what they did with the house."

Bradford nodded. "I spoke to the trustee. He has instructions for how to allocate the assets and part of it includes meeting with you in person."

"Here?"

"In Florida."

"When?"

"As soon as you can get down there."

Levi tensed again. Emotion darkened his eyes when he looked down into mine. "I didn't have much in the bank before I started covering for Ollie at Little Willie's. That's a business that operates in the red. I've been covering the bills while he's been gone. I want to tell you I'll fly both of us down there, but I'm not sure I can swing even one ticket. Now, if you want to drive with me, I'd love for you to be there."

"Hold on." Bradford's voice boomed. "You've been paying Ollie's bills?"

"Someone had to, and we all agreed when Ollie's father died that his mother would never know how expensive it is to keep that place open. It feeds those who can afford to pay and those who can't."

I smiled with pride at Levi. "I was wondering if Ollie was

sending money back or if you were covering for him. You should have said something. I could have chipped in."

Levi shook his head. "I was happy to do it. They've given me so much over the years. I only mentioned it because if I hadn't done that I could have flown you down there and we could have made a vacation out of it." His eyes misted. "Are you sure you don't want to hitch your dreams to a man with more in the bank?"

When I looked back, I'd remember that as the moment I fell in love with Levi. He was strong enough to care for those around him, kindhearted enough to give his last dollar to those in need, and so humble he couldn't see how that made him the only man I could imagine myself with. I threw my arms around his neck and pulled his face to mine, hungrily kissing him with all the emotions flooding through me. When I broke off the kiss, I said, "You foolish, foolish man, how can you not see that you don't need to have money to be everything I want?"

He swept me up in his arms and kissed me again.

In the background, Joanna said, "Now I'm crying."

When he put me down, we were both breathing raggedly and staring into each other's eyes. I wiped happy tears from my cheeks. "Let's drive to Florida and see what that lawyer says. I have a little money set aside, but we'll save it to celebrate with when we hear that the house is yours."

"You're on," he said with a warm smile.

"No," Bradford cut in. "I'll get you both to Florida."

Levi seemed to be flying on the same emotional high as I was when he smiled at Bradford and said, "No offense, but I want to make it nice for Katie."

Bradford's eyebrows rose. "What is that supposed to mean?"

Rubbing a hand along his jaw, Levi took his time answering. "I am grateful for everything you've taught me—as I'm sure Katie is as well."

"Absolutely," I gushed.

"But?" Bradford's eyes narrowed.

Levi's smile turned slightly apologetic. "I've lost count of how many times you've told me to know my strengths as well as my weaknesses. You are exceptionally good at beating down someone to build them up. You're fearless. Dedicated. Ruthless when you need to be."

"But?" he echoed.

My eyes widened. Even I wasn't sure where Levi was going with this.

"You're not Clay when it comes to making things nice."

Joanna's mouth rounded before she brought a hand up to cover it. I felt like I might sprain my neck as I looked back and forth between Levi and Bradford as things began to escalate.

Between gritted teeth, Bradford demanded, "For example?"

Levi's smile didn't waver. "Have you spoken to Clay about Ollie's training?"

"Briefly." Bradford frowned. "He said it went well. Ollie seemed happy enough with it."

Levi laughed and suddenly I knew exactly what he was thinking. I smiled. "I'm sure he was," I said.

Bradford shot me a quick look. "What don't I know?" Oh, the glare. If there was anything Bradford didn't like it was not having all the intel.

With humor in his eyes, Levi said, "Remember when I was fencing your whole ranch and you were beating the shit out of me on the daily?"

Bradford neither agreed nor disagreed with that assessment of his training style.

Levi continued, "Clay had Ollie working out in exclusive gyms, hearing business strategies from billionaires, learning to fly a helicopter, and swimming in the Mediterranean to relax." When Bradford remained quiet, Levi added, "It's not a competition, and I understand that you're not rich like Clay, but I'm imagining you sending Katie and me down to Florida in the back of a shipping container to toughen us up and, although I appreciate the thought, my truck would be much more comfortable."

Bradford brought a fist to his mouth. "First of all, no one is rich like Clay." Before Levi had a chance to respond, Bradford said, "Second, Clay knows nothing about training anyone for anything."

Bringing both hands up in surrender, Levi was still smiling. "Like I said, it's not a competition. Sure, Ollie will come out of this well-dressed with his own business and the connections to ensure its success, but I have a broken nose, Navy SEAL friends, and if Ollie needs to fence-in a parking lot, I'm not only good at it now, but will give him a great price."

Bradford looked down at his wife and grumbled, "Fucking Clay. Do you hear this shit? He always has to one-up me."

Joanna had both sympathy and laughter in her eyes when she said, "His way isn't better; it's just different. You heard Levi. He's grateful, he would just like to pass on traveling in a shipping container."

"You think this is funny?" Bradford growled, but there was no bite to his voice.

She pinched the air. "A little bit."

When he turned back to Levi, he said, "There is nothing Clay could do for someone that I couldn't. We'd just go about it in different ways." He sighed, then demanded, "You want to go to Florida in style? Have a fancy little vacation while you're there? I can not only make that happen, but I can go with you to see that lawyer. People tend to get straight to the point when I'm there."

I didn't have to ask if Levi was going to accept the offer. Without saying a word, he asked me if it was okay if he turned Bradford down and I nodded. Levi had been enjoying giving Bradford shit, but he wasn't looking for a free ride anywhere. Nor was I.

Aloud, Levi said, "Clay's way wasn't better. I'm sure Ollie struggled as well—he said he even had a callous from climbing on and off a yacht." In response to Bradford's glare, Levi turned serious. "Bradford, all joking aside, you don't have to do anything. Katie and I will figure it out."

"Not going to happen," Bradford barked. "Your business with me is not finished. If Clay thinks he can do this better than I can, he's about to see how wrong he is. You want your own business? I'll make sure that happens for you. When I'm done with you and Katie, Ollie will wish he had your connections."

I interjected, "You do know we love Ollie, right?"

Joanna waved a hand. "This isn't about Ollie. This is the pissing contest Bradford and Clay get into every once in a while. Bradford, if you do this, make sure you're doing it for the right reason."

"Does it matter as long as everyone benefits?"

I couldn't hold back. "Actually, it does. My mother is convinced Driverton is entertainment for you and your rich friends. I've told her you all actually care about us. I don't want to be a pawn in some game you're playing with Clay—not even if I get a nice trip out of it."

Joanna walked over and put an arm around me. "Bradford, you tell her right now that you care about her and Levi."

He threw his hands up in the air. "I've spent nearly every day for the past two months with them. How is that not evidence that I care?"

My cheeks warmed. That was a good point. I turned to my best friend for assistance. "Levi, help me out here."

Levi looked around at each of us, then said, "I think what Katie is trying to say is that if you were asking us to do this as a favor for you, we'd be all in. But if it's not framed that way, it feels icky."

Joanna added, "Because these are good people, Bradford. Remember why we moved here? They have integrity, and they're too proud to take handouts or be manipulated. So, why don't you ask them if they'll help you outshine Clay this time?" When he didn't immediately do it, she said, "Bradford has difficulty asking for help."

"Bradford can hear you," Bradford said, but a smile was spreading across his face. "You are correct that I should be more mature than this."

"Go on," Joanna said with humor.

"But clearly, since I am not, Levi and Katie, would you please help me put whatever Clay is doing for Ollie to shame? And make it appear like we'd always planned it this way?"

Levi and I exchanged a look. I said, "As long as it in no way takes away from the good that is happening for Ollie."

"It won't," Bradford promised. "If anything, it'll likely only get Clay to do more for him."

I answered the question in Levi's eyes with a nod. He said, "We're in."

Joanna hopped with excitement next to me. "If we're doing this, I say we go *big*. Bradford, do you remember that card you received when you found that senator's son? The one that just has a phone number you're supposed to call if you ever need anything? What if you called it for this—just to see who answers and what they can do?"

Bradford grinned. "I like the way you think, Joanna. It also adds a level of intrigue to this. Even Clay doesn't know who that number goes to. Genius."

"So, what do we need to do?" I asked.

"I'll send you information tonight," Bradford said, "but have a bag packed and be ready to leave in the morning."

Chapter Twenty-Two

Levi

THE NEXT MORNING, I handed Katie's luggage as well as my duffle bag to the driver Bradford had sent to pick us up. After depositing our things into the trunk of an SUV stretch limo, he returned to hold the door open for us.

Katie went first, choosing to sit in the seat along the back. I settled in beside her, loving how she naturally moved closer. After the driver explained which button we should press if we had any need to communicate with him, he closed the door, and we were alone.

Hand on my thigh, Katie smiled up at me. "Do you remember all of us riding in a limo together to prom because Ollie was dating that rich girl from Holeb?"

I kissed her temple. "I do. You wore a skimpy dress that both Ollie and I thought you shouldn't be allowed to wear, but instead of saying anything to you, we threatened the life of your date if he even thought about touching you."

She laughed. "You didn't."

"We did and we meant it."

"Well, no wonder I didn't even get a kiss at the end of the night. I thought he didn't like me."

"Oh, he liked you. He just liked his appendages unbroken more."

She shook her head but appeared more amused than bothered by the revelation. "That dress was completely in fashion. And expensive. Do you know how long I had to save up to afford it?"

"I didn't say you weren't beautiful in it. You were too young to realize how stupid teenage boys can get around a dress like that."

She gave me an odd look. "I never had a problem with that—well, not until . . ." Her mouth rounded. "Hold on, was there anyone else you and Ollie threatened for me?"

I held back a guilty smile. "I plead the fifth."

She slapped my thigh playfully. "You stinkers. This explains so much. My first choice for prom that year was Joel Hartman. I even asked him when he didn't ask me and now his answer makes sense. He said, 'I wish I were brave enough to say yes.' I just assumed he had high anxiety."

I looked away, then back. "Sorry, not sorry."

Her answering smile was infectious. "If you weren't so good in bed, I'd resent the years of sex you likely cost me, but I suppose you'll just have to make it up to me by continuing to put out."

I growled my approval into the curve of her neck. "I'll do

my best."

"Your best is not so bad." Humor lit her eyes.

Not able to let her get away with that, I turned and lifted her so she faced me, straddling my lap. "Not so bad?" My hands slid down her back, cupping her ass and drawing her forward until she settled intimately on my hardened cock.

She wriggled against me, making it damn near impossible to think of anything but burying myself inside her. "Is that so?"

Her uninhibited laugh was a sheer delight. Being with her was effortless and healing in a way I hadn't known was possible. Was *this* love? It sure as hell was at a whole different level than anything I'd experienced before. I tried and failed to imagine wanting to bring anyone else on a trip full of so many unknowns. There was no one I trusted the way I trusted her. She was my person.

I had a person.

Someone I could imagine sticking by me through the good and bad.

Me.

I wrapped my arms around her and hugged her to my chest so tightly she protested with a laugh. When I released her, she framed my face with her hands. "Are you okay?"

I nodded. When I spoke, my voice betrayed how deeply I felt my next words. "I love you, Katie."

Tears filled her eyes. "I love you too."

"We're doing this."

She nodded and sniffed. "Yes, we are."

"I don't care if we come back from this trip with nothing as long as we come back together."

A tear rolled down her cheek even as a huge smile stretched her lips. "That sure doesn't sound like nothing."

I held her gaze. "You know what I mean. No matter what we find in Florida, I want you to know you'll have that house you want in Driverton—if not the one I live in now, then one we buy or build. We'll make it happen."

"You and me." And I'd never heard sweeter words.

She met my kiss halfway, and as our mouths claimed each other, I saw my future with her and it was full of love, laughter, kids, and chaos. Kids. Had anyone asked me before Katie if I wanted any I would have vehemently denied the possibility that I ever would. I didn't exactly have the best parental role models. Part of me had feared that since I couldn't care enough to stay with any one woman, I also lacked the ability to care enough to stay with any children I might have.

Katie was changing not only how I viewed relationships, but also how I viewed myself. As someone who'd seen firsthand the betrayal of broken promises, I'd be careful never to make any I didn't feel I could keep.

I wasn't afraid to promise Katie anything because her dreams, safety, and happiness mattered more to me than my own. It was unsettling to realize how they always had.

I was in the middle of telling myself that stripping her

bare and taking her right then and there in the back of the limo was a heady temptation I needed to resist when her hands slid down and undid my belt.

Chapter Twenty-Three

Katie

MY FACE WAS still flushed and my hair slightly askew as I stepped out of the limo onto the tarmac of a private airfield. Levi took my hand when he joined me and, as we looked into each other's eyes, I felt at peace with the world. My best friend had just said he loved me—and had shown every inch of me just how much he did. I'm sure I looked as smitten and sexed up as I was. I would have been embarrassed by how obvious we'd been, but it was impossible to be while also feeling so damn good.

"Now that is what I call flying in style," the driver said with a whistle, kindly acting as if he were unaware we'd just rocked the back end of the limo.

"Mr. Hale. Miss Berber. Welcome. My name is Lindsey and it's my pleasure to make sure you have whatever will make this flight the most pleasant for you."

We turned in unison to greet her. She was a tall redhead dressed in a beige pantsuit that looked stylish without being flashy. My attention was drawn past her, though, as I took in the sheer size of the airplane we'd parked beside as well as the bold lettering on its side: *Corisi*. "Thank you," I said breathlessly as a burst of anticipation hit me. "I've never flown anywhere before. Are we late or early?"

"Perfectly on time," she said smoothly.

Levi placed a hand on my lower back and asked, "Where are the other passengers?"

After directing our driver to hand the luggage to another staff member, she smiled at us. "There are no other passengers. This is a private flight for the two of you."

My jaw dropped open as I looked the plane over again. It was the size of a commercial airliner. "No."

"Yes," she answered easily.

"Corisi?" Levi asked as he looked the large plane over. "I've never heard of that airline."

Lindsey brought a hand to her mouth as if to hide a smile. "It belongs to Dominic Corisi. He asked us to pass along that he is looking forward to meeting you while you're down in Florida."

"I don't know that name." Chewing my bottom lip, I looked at Levi. "Do you?"

Levi shrugged. "I recognize it, but I'm unsure where I've heard it. Maybe he's a friend of Bradford's?"

"That must be it," Lindsey said with a blank expression. "If you'd follow me, I'll give you a little tour before we take off."

"A tour?" I'd seen the inside of large planes online, even some private planes. I couldn't imagine one involving more than her pointing to the front where the pilot would be and the rear for a toilet—but, okay.

In my ear, Levi said, "Bradford wasn't kidding when he said he wanted to outshine Clay."

As we followed Lindsey up the stairway to the door of the plane, I said, "He sure wasn't. Can you believe this is a private plane? Whoever Dominic Corisi is, he must be loaded."

"Or broke after buying this," Levi said. "I'm sure it wasn't cheap."

How much of an understatement that was became clear as soon as we stepped inside. To the left, there was a door I assumed led to the cockpit or a galley; it was the opulence of the room that unfolded before us that took my breath away. It was ultramodern with a long built-in couch on one side, individual seating on the other, as well as a dining room table on the other end of it. "Wow," I whispered. Levi stayed at my side.

Lindsey motioned for us to follow her. "If you're tired, there are two small bedrooms off the main that you could use, each with a shower. The Jacuzzi can be filled and heated if you feel that you'd like to use it, although this is a relatively short flight. The theater is past the bedrooms down this hallway. If the movie is out, we can pull it up. If it hasn't been released yet, but production is completed, I may need a few minutes to contact the studio to have the file sent over, but don't hesitate to request those titles as well."

"You're serious?" Levi asked.

Without batting an eyelash, Lindsey responded, "Of course. The comfort and satisfaction of his guests are always important to Mr. Corisi. Few requests are denied unless immoral or generally considered distasteful."

I looked around, eyes still wide with wonder. "I can't imagine what we'd even ask for. Maybe just a water? Or Sprite if you have some."

"I'd like a water too," Levi said. "Thank you."

"I'll be right back with some." She motioned for us to follow her to the main room where we chose to sit side by side in chairs with seatbelts. She returned with glass bottles of water as well as glasses filled with ice then placed them on a table she pulled out from the wall. "Is there anything else I could get you?"

I shrugged. Levi mirrored my move.

Rather than walking away as expected, she leaned in with a smile. "Tell me if you'd rather be left alone for the flight, but I have the feeling neither of you are aware of how wonderful this flight could be. If you'd allow me the pleasure of setting up a few things for you, and about thirty minutes to have the resources arrive, I'd love to make this flight extra special."

The genuineness of her smile made it easy to trust her. I glanced at Levi in question and saw that we agreed, so I said,

"We're not in a hurry—so, if it's not too much trouble for you, sure. We're okay with waiting."

"Relax, then. I'll be back in a few minutes."

Levi stood. "Lindsey?"

She paused. "Yes, Mr. Hale."

"Thank you in advance. For whatever it is you're planning. It's appreciated."

Her head tipped to the side. "You're very welcome." After giving us each a long look, she smiled again and walked away.

He retook his seat beside me. "Sorry, I might have just made that awkward, but I wanted this trip to be nice for you and hearing that she was going to do something special for us . . ."

"You're amazing, do you know that?" My hand tightened on his. This, this was one of the many reasons I loved Levi. Life could have left him bitter and ungrateful, but it hadn't. Yes, he was strong and resilient, but also attentive to the needs of others and bold when it came to making sure those around him felt valued. He'd make an incredible father and one I could imagine proudly hosting pretend tea parties for our future children. There wasn't anything he wouldn't do for those he loved.

"It comes and goes." His smile was humble and oh, so sexy. "But you bring out the best in me."

"Same," I said with what was becoming a perma-smile. It was amazing how much my life had changed even though very little actually had. Driverton remained where I wanted to live, Levi was still my best friend, and my bank account didn't yet reflect any of the work I'd put into improving myself. And yet, every part of my life was better . . . filled with more promise . . . and hope. The past and any mistakes I'd made no longer weighed me down. I felt free to start over. "I don't care how many women you've been with as long as I'm the last one."

His eyebrows rose in surprise, but he nodded. "I can do that."

Although he said the words with confidence, I had to ask, "Can you? Don't say it if you're not sure."

He frowned and I wasn't sure how to take the pause before he spoke. In the time it took him to choose his next words, I'd imagined all sorts of horrible possibilities, as I held my breath and waited. "You're my person."

It wasn't so much what he said but how he said it that left me with no doubt he meant it with every fiber of him. I gulped in air while nodding vigorously before saying, "How did it take us this long to figure out that we belong together?"

With one hand caressing the side of my face, he said, "We weren't ready. I still had a lot of stupid to outgrow."

I chuckled at that. "You did."

He kissed me then said, "A kinder response would have been to deny I did."

"But that wouldn't have been honest. We've both done a

lot of growing this year." I searched his face, suddenly serious. "I love how well we know each other and how much we've shared."

His grin was lopsided. "You may know *too much* about me."

"You're right. Do you know how much you spilled to me whenever you were shitfaced?"

"No. I don't remember doing that." His forehead furrowed again.

I gave his hand a supportive squeeze. "That's the point. It was only when you were really out of it that you'd share whatever was bothering you."

After a pause, he asked, "What kind of things did I tell you?"

"It's the sober friend's duty to forget that kind of stuff the next day."

"No, seriously, tell me."

Still, I hedged. "You trusted me in a way you didn't trust even Ollie. I was someone you felt wouldn't judge you or bring it up the next day. It wouldn't feel right to betray drunk Levi, not even now."

"You do know that drunk Levi and sober Levi are the same person."

"I do."

His face tightened. "Drunk me never . . . I never offended you . . . or . . ."

"Oh, my God, no," I rushed to assure him. "No matter

how drunk you were, you were never inappropriate. Not with me. And as far as I know, not with anyone else. You'd just get sad."

"Sad?" He groaned.

He wasn't going to stop until I told him. "You would tell me how much you still loved your parents even though you hated them for leaving. Sometimes you'd tell me about the women you were sleeping with and how shitty you felt about yourself because you wanted to care about them but couldn't because . . ."

"Because?"

I swallowed hard. Did he really want to know I knew? "Because you were afraid that no one would ever love you enough to stay."

He cleared his throat. "That's . . ."

"Understandable."

"I was going to say pathetic."

"I never saw it that way." I stood and sat sideways across his lap, resting my head on his chest, and hoping he could feel how much I loved him. "You trusted me enough to let me in and those talks felt like a precious gift you entrusted me to care for. You even talked to me about Mary a few times and how you wanted to be with her because she had a perfect life and you wanted to see what that was like. When you told me you didn't love her, but that you were going to propose to her, I warned you that you were about to make a huge mistake. You said you didn't think you could stop yourself and I told you that you were better than that. I didn't want to see Mary hurt and that's what you would have done had you not proposed to her mother instead."

He wrapped his arms around me. "Looks like Ollie was right. It was a delib-cident."

"A what?"

"An accident a person does deliberately to get out of doing something they know they shouldn't." He hugged me closer. "Sober me took the advice a good friend gave drunk me. Thank you."

I breathed him in. "You're welcome. Sorry, Mary, not sorry."

He chuckled. "How can you know so much about me and still love me?"

I looked up at him through my lashes. "I could easily ask you the same question." Okay, it was a shameless ploy to get him to talk more about what still felt too good to be true to me. People liked me. Men liked me. But I'd doubted I'd ever find the kind of love my parents had.

Holding my gaze he said, "I've always admired how you own your journey. You've never tried to pretty it up or rewrite it. That's why I've always appreciated when you've held me accountable for my shit. You weren't judging me; you were pushing me to be a better version of myself and I needed that."

"I've always been grateful for how you jump to my defense even when I'm wrong then help me see the situation differently later when I've had time to cool off. I never felt, not one single day of my life, that I'd have to go into a battle alone. You were always there—watching out for me. I needed that."

"God, we're fucking wonderful."

I burst out laughing at that. "We're something, that's for sure."

His eyes darkened. "I believe in you, and in me when I'm with you."

My throat thickened with emotion. "That had better be in your marriage vows to me."

Smiling, he said, "I love that I never have to wonder what you want."

I pinched him, then whispered in his ear, "Then I should tell you that I'm hoping that part of what Lindsey considers making this flight special is giving us some time alone in that Jacuzzi."

"I believe that can be arranged."

Chapter Twenty-Four

Levi

A SHORT TIME later, after a long soak in the Jacuzzi, Katie and I were laid out on side-by-side portable massage tables in one of the guest bedrooms. No one was allowed in the owner's suite, which I completely respected. Equipped with a bed, a large enough open area for the massage tables to be set up, as well as a full bathroom with a shower, there was more than enough for any guest to feel pampered.

It was my first professional massage and although I would have preferred Katie's touch to the man kneading my back muscles, I had to admit it was relaxing. Soft music filled the room and every once in a while Katie would raise her head to smile at me.

We were both nude beneath the sheets they'd instructed us to cover ourselves with. The experience wasn't overtly sexual, but it was a pleasurable experience we were exploring together. I loved watching her enjoy it more than I cared for my own massage. The man working on me seemed to completely understand because he didn't ask me to change my position when I kept my head raised to soak in the view of my woman.

Eyes closed, Katie murmured, "This is so nice. I'm glad we chose the hot stones."

"Me too," I answered. It took very little to make Katie happy, but I wanted so much more for her. Funny how my perspective of everything, the past as well as the future, was changing the more I gave myself over to being with Katie.

Trust didn't come easily to me, nor did optimism, but I needed both to be the man Katie deserved. There weren't too many job opportunities in Driverton, but I'd figure out something when we returned. It would likely mean working full-time with Bradford or one of his friends, but if that allowed me to build a financially stable life with Katie— that's what I'd do.

I'd discovered an unexpected side-effect of making her happiness a priority to me. Suddenly, the possibility of true happiness for myself felt attainable.

It involved letting go of things I'd held on to for too long.

And reaching for goals I'd never allowed myself to believe I was worthy of.

Trust—not just in her and others, but in myself and my ability to heal.

I'd considered myself too broken for her or anyone else.

What I was beginning to see was that every hit I'd taken,

every fracture that had healed, had made me stronger. I was no longer afraid of learning that my parents might have been happier without me or that they might have harbored some horrific secret. I was stronger than the teenage boy they'd left behind. Who they were and what they had done no longer had the power to define who I was.

The woman who'd been working on Katie said, "Unless you'd like to extend your session, we'll end here. There's time for a nap and a shower before we land."

"I can't imagine ever moving again," Katie joked without raising her head.

I nodded my appreciation toward both massage therapists. They didn't require more than that to quietly leave us.

Rising from my table, I stood beside Katie's and began to gently massage her shoulders. She turned her head toward me and murmured, "It's like you can read my mind. I was imagining your hands on me."

I pulled the sheet off with one powerful move and dropped it to the floor. Every glorious inch of her backside was oiled and glistening. I moved my hands up and down her back in a more sensual version of the massage we'd received. My hands didn't stop at the dip of her back but moved down to knead her buttocks and caress her inner thighs. She parted her legs for me, allowing my fingers full access to her wet sex. I teased. Circled. Dipped inside of her. She was a feast laid out for me that I explored first with my hands but craved to taste as well.

I turned her over and kissed her deeply while working my fingers in and out of her. God, she was perfection, jutting eagerly, wantonly against my hand. Her mouth wasn't enough for me. I tasted my way down her neck, then savored one breast before indulging in the other. It was good, but I wanted more. I moved to the end of the table, hooked my hands below each of her knees and pulled her forward, pushing her legs upward as I did, then spreading them wide in the air.

When I bent and claimed her sex with my mouth, her legs began to lower onto my shoulders, but I corrected that with a light slap to the sides of her ass cheeks. Her response was to straighten them then dig her hands into my hair and thrust herself more fully against my tongue. We were beyond asking each other for what we wanted. We took as much as we gave, and it was hot as hell.

I brought her to the brink of an orgasm and stopped. She grasped wildly at me as I pulled away but cried out my name with pleasure when I thrust my engorged cock deeply within her. Her hair was splayed out across the table and her breasts bounced wildly as I drove into her with a fierceness I normally held back. This was my woman. Her cries for me to not stop, to go harder, deeper—echoed how I needed this fuck to be. I was promising her all of me, demanding she promise me the same. And she was. We came together with a wildness that left us both breathless and shaken.

After withdrawing from her, I helped her to a seated position, lifted her into my arms and carried her to the shower. Beneath the warm spray of water, I gently washed her, and when she smiled at me with wonder, I knew this was what people meant when they said two could become one. No matter where life took us or what challenges it offered up, we would always have each other.

I felt that truth to my very core.

Chapter Twenty-Five

Katie

A SHORT TIME later, Levi and I stood in our underwear next to a large closet. I waved a paper at him. "The note says the clothing is for us. A gift."

Levi made a face. "I'm comfortable in jeans."

I replaced the note on the table beside the closer. "Me too." I'd never been fancy. Still, I reached out and chose a cream-colored, button-down linen dress. "Do you think this is what rich people wear?"

He shrugged. "I'm sure they wear whatever they want to."

I held the dress up to the front of me. "It feels wrong to not at least try one outfit on."

"Criminal."

Enthusiasm began to build in me. "Don't make me do this alone. You have to try one on too."

His eyebrows arched. "Try on a dress?"

Laughing, I handed him brown trousers. "Or these. I'm

sure they can still return the clothing if all we do is try them on. We could have our own fashion show. What do you think?"

Humor lit his eyes. "You could talk me into anything today." He took the trousers and stepped into them.

I slid the dress over my head, loving how he helped the material over my hips as naturally as if we were an old married couple. I handed him a striped shirt even though, bare-chested and beefed up, he looked like a photo ad for those trousers.

"Beautiful," he murmured as he looked me over.

"You're not so bad yourself," I answered with a smile as I gave him an equally long inspection.

We turned in unison and posed in front of the mirror, both laughing, and the image of us together and happy nearly had me breathless for a moment. There was no going back to how we'd been. I could no longer imagine us not like this.

Although I'd never been happier, there was an element to our trip that we were both avoiding talking about: the reason for it. Not knowing what we'd discover in Florida had to be weighing on him.

"Hey," he said, turning to face me. "What's wrong?"

I raised a hand and caressed his strong jaw. "How are you holding up?" When he looked about to pacify me by saying he was fine, I added, "Be honest. I'm having a wonderful time, but this is hard for you, isn't it?"

The walls he kept up for others lowered. "It is, but you're with me and that makes everything survivable."

"How do you do it?" I blinked back tears. "How do you make me love you more every single day?"

"I could ask you the same thing." He brought my hand to his mouth and kissed it, but there was sadness in his eyes. "There's a possibility that my parents were happier without me in their lives."

I gripped his hand tightly. "Don't say that."

He pulled me into the circle of his arms and tucked my head beneath his chin. I cuddled against him, soothed by the steady beat of his heart. "I'm hoping to hear something good, but I'm prepared for the worst. They never came back for me, never sent news that they were okay. If I don't allow for the possibility that they simply didn't care enough to let me know, none of this makes sense."

"They were the broken ones, not you. No matter what we uncover—you were a child when they left. You didn't create whatever was wrong with them, and it wasn't your responsibility to fix them." I wrapped my arms around his waist and hugged him with all of my might.

"I know."

I tipped my head back so I could look him in the eye. "Don't know it—believe it. Not because I'm telling you to, and we both know how often I'm right, but because it's the truth."

"Thank you." His smile started in his eyes then spread

across his face. "Now for the important question we both need to answer."

I crooked my head to the side in question.

He continued, "What should we wear to this potential shit-show?"

I stepped back and did a little twirl before him. "I kind of love this dress. Maybe we could offer to buy it?"

"I'll speak to Lindsey. I'm sure we can."

After looking him up and down, I said, "Those pants are a must, but try on the blue Oxford."

He chuckled. "You just want to see me shirtless again."

I answered coyly, "Maybe?"

He turned, pulled a tiny red dress out of the closet, and held it up. "I'll try on the blue shirt if you try this dress on."

"You just want to see me strip down for you."

His grin was pure male. "Maybe?"

Feeling young, beautiful, and playful, I began to unbutton my dress. "I may need to see you in the gray pullover as well."

When I stood before him in my underwear, with the red dress in one hand, he reached behind me and released my bra snap. I let it fall to the floor. In that deep voice he used when he was turned on, he growled, "That little dress needs the right accessories." With that he bent his head and took one of my nipples between his teeth, tugging gently on it, while flicking back and forth against the tip of it with his tongue. It puckered and hardened. He moved on to the other and did the same before slipping the dress over my head.

The thin material clung to my excited nipples, accentuating them. His cheeks flushed as he looked down at them with pleasure and brought his thumbs up to circle them. "Beautiful."

My breathing turned ragged as I fought to remain coherent. "So, this one instead?"

He raised his gaze to mine. "No. This one is for my eyes only." He pulled me forward and against his prominent erection. "Just like you. Mine."

Had any other man said that to me, I would have told him I was an independent woman who didn't need or want to belong to anyone. That wasn't how I felt at all with Levi. I wanted to be his. I wanted him to be mine.

If he ordered me to drop to my knees right then and take him in my mouth—I would have done so without hesitation. Submission to him was empowering because I knew I could ask him to drop to his knees and he would—eagerly. Levi had proven time and time again that I was his priority.

When I flicked my tongue across my bottom lip, his eyes dilated. No request was needed. I unbuttoned the front of his trousers and freed his cock. He inhaled sharply as I lowered myself before him and began to love him with my mouth.

He dug his hands into my hair and murmured, "You give the best pep talks."

I laughed and nearly choked on the length of him. I

would have tossed back something witty then, but instead just circled his tip with my tongue and enjoyed the moan that elicited from him.

Pep talk? I kind of like calling it that—for when he'd pleasure me as well.

Hon, I'm feeling a little stressed about going grocery shopping today. I think I need a pep talk.

Yes, I could see me using that term often in the future.

Chapter Twenty-Six

Levi

I WAS FEELING at one with the universe by the time Katie and I were seated in the main cabin as the plane prepared for landing. She looked stunning in the original cream dress she'd tried on. Per her request, I was in a pair of expensive trousers and the gray pullover she chose for me. We'd decided to keep one outfit each. Not only had Lindsey refused to tell us how much we should pay her for the clothing, but she'd said if there was any further mention of payment for them our host would be offended. When we protested, she equated it to offering to pay for a bottle of wine a guest brings to your house as a gift. Although I didn't see it as the same thing at all, neither Katie nor I wanted to seem ungrateful to someone who'd been so generous. I'd just have to find a way to repay him in the future.

The plane was still descending when Lindsey chose a seat across from us and buckled herself in. "I hope you both enjoyed the flight."

In a gush, Katie said, "Oh, my gosh, it flew by, and everything was so perfect. I don't even know how to thank you. I didn't bring much cash with me, but should we tip you? We could send you something when we land. Or is there a benefit for you if we leave you a good review? I don't know how any of this works, but you were amazing, and I'd love to do something amazing for you."

I took one of Katie's hands in mine and gave it a squeeze then looked at Lindsey as well. "I feel the same. This isn't an easy trip for us, but you made it special and if there's anything we can do to repay that—tell us what it is."

Lindsey crossed one leg over the other and tapped her nails on the armrest. "I don't like many people, but I like the two of you."

Katie and I exchanged a look. With humor, I said, "Thanks?"

Her expression lost some of its humility. "When Bradford called me and asked me to help you, I agreed mostly out of curiosity."

I didn't know how to respond to that, so I waited. Katie seemed to make the same decision.

Lindsey reached into a pocket and pulled out a black card with just a phone number written on it and held it out to me. "This is the number he called. It's the only way to reach me. Normally I tell a person to only call it in case of an emergency."

I accepted the card, showed it to Katie, then pocketed it.

"I hope we never have a need to. Would you like our numbers . . . in case you ever find yourself in Maine and in need of help?"

Her lips pressed together as if she were in on a joke we weren't. "No need, I have your information, but I appreciate the offer." After a moment, she added, "You should know, I'm not really a flight attendant."

My hand tightened on Katie's, and I tensed, readying myself for whatever she was about to share. This woman, whoever she was, must know I would do anything to protect Katie. I hoped she didn't test that. "Who are you?" I demanded.

Katie leaned forward and laid her other hand on my forearm. "I don't understand."

"Are you still clueless regarding who Dominic Corisi is?" the woman asked. "You didn't feel the need to Google his name?"

My face flushed. Considering that we were on his plane, I probably should have, but I'd had other things on my mind. Katie in the Jacuzzi. Katie in the shower. What we might discover in Florida. Katie with her mouth wrapped around my cock. In a tight voice, I answered, "No."

"Should we have?" Katie asked in an anxious voice that made me feel a little guilty for where my thoughts had just taken me. "What don't we know?"

I took out my phone and typed in the name from the side of the plane. "Oh," was all I said as I read the results that came up. "Billionaire Tech Giant, Dominic Corisi", "American Royalty? Meet the Corisis." "Rich, Powerful and Not in the News? How Dominic Corisi dominates from the shadows."

Katie turned my phone so she could see the results as well. "So, he's like Clay Landon."

Lindsey laughed. "Oh, sweetie, they could not be less similar, and I don't suggest you voice that comparison to Dominic."

Losing patience, I said, "As much as we appreciate all you've done, if your goal is to intimidate us, you should know it won't work. Money doesn't impress us. We never had any money, don't need much, don't resent people who have more. We're happy with our lives and don't care how you live yours."

Katie added, "We're also well-trained in self-defense. Okay, Levi is more than I am. I'm better at picking locks and hostage negotiation. But the point is, together, we're a formidable team."

"No wonder I like you." Lindsey nodded with approval. "Not only could I work with you two, but I feel like I *have to*. I like what Bradford is trying to do in Driverton. Dominic does as well. Clay can't take your secret project to the next level, but we can. And we will."

"Are we supposed to know what that means?" I asked.

Still far too amused with herself, she shook her head. "No. Not yet. But you will." She pointed toward the runway we were approaching. "See the security down there? That's a sliver of what you will encounter today. Dominic flew to Florida to meet you. That's a bigger deal than you're likely to understand now, but he's asked me to bring you to him at his oceanfront home."

Alone, I wouldn't have had a problem going, but I wasn't about to bring Katie into a situation I didn't know was safe. "And if we say no?"

"I don't remember the last time someone said no to Dominic, but I wouldn't suggest it." She gave me a long look then sighed. "You have nothing to fear. In fact, if you charm the Corisis like you've charmed me, you'll never have to look over your shoulder because no one would dare mess with you."

Katie cleared her throat and in a polite tone said, "We can give the clothes back. I think it's safe to say that neither of us are actively trying to charm anyone."

The plane bounced as we landed. I released my seatbelt and stood, placing myself protectively in front of Katie. "Please tell Mr. Corisi that, although we appreciate his generosity, we'll be finding our own way back to Maine."

Lindsey laughed. "Stop. I'm sorry. I've done this poorly. I'm just not used to people having no idea who Dominic is. Had I known how adorable the two of you would be I would have filmed these conversations. Seriously, Marc will think I'm exaggerating when I tell him how wholesome you are."

Katie came to stand at my side and laced her hand with

mine. I knew before she spoke what she was going to say and didn't try to stop her. "Lindsey—"

"My real name is Alethea Stone."

"Alethea," Katie continued, "you're making it difficult to like or trust you. We want to do both. If you stop laughing at us and just tell us what you feel we don't understand about this situation, we could make an informed decision. We don't meet many new people, so maybe we're doing this poorly as well, but to be blunt, you're being a bit of an ass."

All amusement left Alethea's face. "Well, aren't you a bold one."

I rose to my full height at that challenge. Woman or not, if she came for Katie, she'd have to come through me.

Katie didn't seem intimidated at all. In fact, the look she was giving Alethea reminded me of the one she often gave me and Ollie. "I said what I said. That doesn't mean we can't be friends. It just means we have standards on how we'll accept being treated. To laugh at us, you must be one of us. And to be one of us, you must be someone we trust. Can we trust you? Because that's what we're trying to figure out."

Expression tight, Alethea said, "Oh, I can be trusted, but be aware that when it comes to people I care about, there's nothing I wouldn't do to protect them."

"Then we have something in common," I said in a low tone.

"It seems that we do." Her eyes narrowed before a smile

returned to her face. "Let's start over, shall we? You don't owe anyone anything for this trip or the gifts you received during it. Bradford located and returned the son of a friend of Dominic's. When he asked me if something could be done to make this trip special for you, I investigated who you are and the little town you're from. I didn't find a single thing I didn't like, so here I am."

Something still felt off. "I'll ask you again, who are you?"

She understood I wasn't asking to hear her name. "My husband and I lead Dominic's security team, but we're also friends of his."

I frowned. "Why would someone like him want to meet *us*?" That's what didn't make sense to me. Billionaires didn't fly anywhere to meet people who had nothing to offer them.

Alethea rose to her feet. "It's not my place to discuss his business, but I can say that if I were in your place, I'd meet with him."

I looked at Katie. "I'll go. You—"

She shook her head. "We rescued Everette together. We do this together too. I'm not afraid of any old stodgy billionaire." She winked. "Not when I've got you."

My chest puffed with male pride. Sure, she was feeding my ego on purpose, but that didn't mean it didn't feel good to know she knew I'd give my life to protect her.

"Stodgy." Alethea coughed.

Deciding to ignore the amusement of a woman I hadn't yet decided what I thought of, I turned my attention back to one who mattered the most to me. "Our appointment with the lawyer is tomorrow morning. I guess we have time to meet a billionaire before we find our hotel."

Katie's face lit up. "It might even be fun—a little adventure."

Alethea laughed and said, "This is so adorable." When I looked at her in annoyance, her smile widened. "Sorry. You're right. I'm being rude." She cleared her throat. "I'll do better."

"I'd say we will too, but this is already us at our best," Katie said in a serious tone, then winked.

I barked out a laugh then nuzzled her neck.

Alethea laughed as well. "I can't wait to see how you get on with Dominic."

Chapter Twenty-Seven

Katie

L EVI AND I had stepped out of reality and into some fairy tale where every door opened before we reached it, and every need was anticipated and addressed before we had a chance to voice it. We rode in a motorcade of black SUVs like we were people of importance.

We were stopped at a red light when our driver, a muscular man in a casual suit, asked, "How was your flight?"

I smiled as a myriad of emotions washed over me in response. The wonder of it all. The great sex. How much I loved Levi. Not knowing if agreeing to meet Dominic Corisi had been a wise choice. "Magical. Amazing. A little unnerving."

"Alethea told me she might have enjoyed meeting you a little too much," the driver said. "She can be a lot initially. She likes to test people—see who they become when she pushes a few of their buttons."

"Sounds like you know her well," I said dryly. Was that

what her condescending humor had been about? A test?

He smiled back at us. "She's my wife."

"Oh," I said as I put those puzzle pieces together. "So, you're not really a driver."

"I play whatever role I'm asked to, but I'll admit that I don't normally drive people around."

That was hard to believe. I glanced at Levi. "She's his wife."

I wanted to ask Levi if he thought it was odd that two unknowns like us were being met by the head of Dominic Corisi's security.

He nodded in response to my unspoken question then asked, "Did we pass or fail her test?"

Without missing a beat, the driver responded, "You're here, aren't you?"

"For now." Levi bent forward and looked out the window at the palm trees that lined the street. "How far is our hotel from where we're going?"

"Not far."

"Should we anticipate any more *tests* before we get there?"

"What's your name?" I asked when the driver didn't immediately answer Levi.

"Marc."

"Marc, we're okay with meeting your boss, but you have to understand that it's not the reason we're here. If we need to prove that we're worthy of that privilege, I think we're both okay with just going to our hotel instead."

"We are," Levi said in a low tone.

Marc's eyebrows rose. "Wait, are you telling me you'd rather not meet Dominic?"

I looked at Levi then met Marc's gaze in the rearview mirror. "It's not a priority."

Levi kissed my temple then added, "Doesn't even make the list of the top ten things we'd like to do while here."

After a moment, Marc smiled. "You're serious?"

In full agreement, we both nodded.

Marc said, "I'm beginning to understand why my wife wanted me to meet you. You're definitely likable. I should warn you that Alethea's curiosity is insatiable. That's only a problem, though, if you're sitting on a secret."

Despite being unsure about the situation, Marc's brag about his wife struck me as funny. "*A secret?* We're from Driverton where everyone not only knows everyone's business but also has an opinion about it that they're not afraid to voice."

"Ain't that the truth." Arm around me, Levi added, "It's a place where breaking a branch from the closest tree is still how you tell a neighbor's kid to stay out of your garden."

"And nearly everyone has felt the sting at least once by Mr. Arnold's rock-salt shotgun."

Levi added, "A rite of passage."

Marc asked, "Why is someone in your town shooting people?"

Levi and I answered in unison, "Plums."

I said, "It's not even about eating them. It's the challenge of seeing if you can get in and out of his orchard without getting caught."

"It usually takes twice," Levi said. "You're overconfident the first time. The second time you're faster."

The driver laughed. "Sounds like a great town."

"It is. And a good place to grow up," I said spontaneously.

Levi added, "As well as to raise a family."

I melted against him. "Because the people there are genuine."

Levi smiled down into my eyes. "And loyal."

"Everyone takes care of everyone else."

"And we might fight amongst ourselves, but if you come for one of us, you'll deal with all of us."

The thoughts welling within me could not remain unspoken. "Which is why it doesn't matter what we do or don't return home with—as long as we return together."

Levi hugged me to his side. "Exactly."

The drive wasn't long, but we traveled the rest of it in silence. When we pulled into a gated driveway that opened when we approached, I clasped my hands on my lap. The house we parked in front of was large enough to be a hotel—two hotels. "How many toilets do you think are in that house?"

Marc answered. "There are twenty-one bedrooms and, I

believe, twenty-eight and a half bathrooms."

"It's beautiful," I said, "but I can't imagine trying to keep it clean."

"They probably have staff," Levi said.

I nodded. "That makes sense."

Marc parked the car then walked around to open the door for us. Taking advantage of the opportunity to speak to Levi alone, I said, "It looks like Dominic Corisi really is wealthy."

Levi smiled reassuringly at me. "You know what they say about men with big houses . . ."

We were both still laughing at that as we stepped out of the car and onto the driveway. We linked hands and I was grateful it was Levi by my side. Had I been there with someone who was easily intimidated I might have been as well. Although several wealthy people had come to Driverton recently, they didn't feel different than us because they were on our turf, living as simply as we were.

Clay probably owned a large house as well. Suddenly, I could understand why my parents felt we were too different to truly be friends. We were not the same. When I tensed, Levi stepped closer to me.

Marc led us up an impressive stone stairway to an ornate wooden door. It opened and I expected to be greeted by a butler, but instead the doorway was filled by a tall man in a dark suit. He had a full head of jet-black hair with a peppering of gray along his temple. His eyes were a striking gray and despite being older than we were, he looked fit enough to hold his own in a fight.

He held out a hand for me to shake. "Miss Berber." I shook his hand vigorously. He then shook Levi's. "Mr. Hale. It's a pleasure to meet both of you. Come in."

I turned to Marc and whispered, "Is that him?"

He seemed to bite back a smile as he nodded.

Hand in hand Levi and I followed Marc who followed Mr. Corisi through a two-story white marble foyer to a living room that looked like it came straight out of a movie set. One entire wall was windows that overlooked a view of a lawn then the ocean. The detail of the ceiling caught my attention, gold design trim over a rich brown. Sets of couches and chairs were organized in different areas. I was reminded of something I'd once heard about how you could tell someone was wealthy by how little of their furniture touched a wall. I hadn't really understood that concept before seeing it at this level. All the women in Driverton could easily gather in this one room and there'd still be space to move about.

Levi spoke first. "Thank you for flying us down—and for everything."

"You're welcome."

We stood in awkward silence. I was tempted to blurt something, anything, but instead took my cue from Levi who seemed to be waiting out the older man.

Dominic motioned toward one of the leather couches.

"Sit. Would either of you like something to eat or drink?"

Levi and I both shook our heads before moving to sit. Once we were settled, Dominic took a seat across from us. Marc moved away to another part of the room.

After a few torturous minutes, Dominic said, "Mr. Hale, what are you doing here in Florida?"

Levi held his gaze steadily. "You already know."

A slight smile stretched Dominic's lips. "I do, but I'd like to hear it from you."

Sitting up straighter, Levi said, "I'm here to find out who my parents left the house I live in to. There's a chance they left it to me. There's a chance they didn't."

"And what about the resort?"

My heart broke for Levi when he said, "There's zero chance they would have left that to me. All I care about is the house and I'm prepared to receive disappointing news about that as well."

Dominic gave us each a long look before saying, "Interesting. We do a full background check on everyone we associate with. When I read yours, you sounded like someone with a lot more fight in him."

Levi inhaled sharply. "Only when it comes to things I care about."

"But you're okay if you lose the house."

Levi's grip on my hand tightened uncomfortably. When I wiggled within his grasp, he instantly loosened his hold. "I'm not okay with anything regarding my parents, but I've learned to have extremely low expectations when it comes to them."

Dominic nodded. "I understand that better than I'd care to admit." He cleared his throat. "Call me Dominic."

Hoping I could ease the tension, I tried to sound cheerful when I said, "Hello, Dominic. You're welcome to call me Katie."

"Levi," was all Levi said.

"Well now that we're on such good terms, let's cut through the niceties, shall we? You two were brought to my attention via a favor requested by someone I owed one to. What are you looking for from me?"

Levi and I glanced at each other, and I took the lead. "You've already done more than enough. Your plane was amazing. We used credit card points to reserve a room in Miami. Tomorrow we'll meet with the lawyer then either book a flight—"

"I'll fly you home, of course."

"Of course," I echoed nervously. All of this was uncharted territory.

Levi said, "That's kind of you."

Dominic crossed his legs at the ankles. "And you'll stay here."

I sputtered, "We couldn't—"

Levi spoke at the same time. "Bradford is meeting us at the hotel and going with us to see the lawyer."

"You'll stay here." Dominic looked across to Marc who

nodded then brought a hand to his ear and began to speak to someone on what I assumed was an earpiece.

Levi stood. "Thank you for your time, Mr. Corisi, but Katie and I will be leaving now."

I rose to stand beside Levi. "We do appreciate everything you've done. It's just that . . ."

Still seated casually, Dominic asked, "Are you afraid to stay here?" When neither of us answered him, he flashed his teeth in a smile.

I let Levi answer that one. He inhaled deeply, then said, "What do you want from us?"

"Honesty," Dominic answered without pause.

"About?" Levi bit out the question.

"Who you both are and what your potential is. On paper, neither of you is that impressive."

Ouch.

He continued, "At first I couldn't understand why someone like Bradford Wilson would waste his time in Driverton training people with no apparent prior skillset."

Neither Levi nor I had a polite response to that, so we kept our thoughts to ourselves.

Dominic said, "But then I heard about how you saved your friend and a stranger from serial killers. That was impressive. So, I dug deeper. Driverton is the perfect cover for a covert, outside-the-law operation. Involving high-profile investors like Clay Landon wasn't wise, though. You invite the possibility of putting your little town on the map."

I felt the need to add, "We're not in charge of who is or

isn't part of anything Bradford does. Honestly, we're just grateful for the opportunity. Work is hard to come by where we are."

Dominic nodded toward Levi. "You turned down more than one lucrative job offer."

That snapped my attention back to Levi. "You did? When? Why?"

Levi looked uncomfortable as he admitted, "Right after my training with Bradford. Both positions would have required me to relocate. My place is in Driverton, with you, making sure no one Bradford pisses off takes it out on the people we love."

I wrapped my arms around his waist and looked proudly up at him. "You're incredible. I hope you know that . . ."

In the background, Dominic said, "I'm in agreement. Not many would have walked away from the kind of money they offered you."

Levi kissed my forehead before answering. "It wasn't a difficult choice to make. Driverton is my home."

And so are you.

He didn't need to say the last words. I saw them in his eyes as he smiled down at me. "You still should have told me, Levi," I said softly. "That's a huge achievement."

He held my gaze. "I'd rather celebrate your wins. Dominic, this woman hasn't met a lock she can't pick."

"Care to prove that?" Dominic asked.

"Not really," I answered, my attention remaining on Levi. "No offense, but my plans don't include working for anyone outside of Driverton, either."

"Marc," Dominic called out.

"Yes?"

"Bring in their lawyer. I need to know how this turns out for them."

"Absolutely," Marc said before stepping out of the living room.

"Don't we have to wait until tomorrow?" I asked, confused.

Levi looked from Dominic to me. "Something tells me Dominic doesn't play by the same rules we do."

Dominic let out a deep laugh. "Never have. Never will."

It only took that short amount of time for Marc to return with a tall man in a gray suit, with thinning hair and spectacles. His skin shone with nervous sweat. Dominic motioned for him to join us, then for us to retake our seats.

The lawyer introduced himself as the executor of the trust. He began to read the document aloud, starting with the grantors of the trust, taxes, and bill payments, then the provision that they left everything to each other in case of death. We collectively held our breath when the lawyer read, "In the event of both of our deaths . . ." My heart was beating so loudly that I wondered if others could hear it.

So much of the legal terminology went over my head, but when he said, "The entirety of the estate shall be distributed to our son and only heir, Levi Hale. This shall include: Sunny Side Up Island, all of the buildings and assets located on it as well as all business and personal cash assets." I nearly burst into tears when the house in Driverton was mentioned and was bequeathed to Levi with the condition that the estate pays off the mortgage in full first."

Unable to contain my excitement, I threw my arms around Levi. "You got the house."

Although his arms wrapped around me, I could tell he was still reeling from the shock of it. "And an island, apparently."

Hearing the pain in his voice, I quelled my excitement. "What do you need?"

Shaking his head, Levi answered. "Just a moment. It's a relief that they left it to me, but . . ."

I hugged him tighter. "I know." I looked over at the lawyer and asked, "Did they leave a letter for him?"

He removed his spectacles then shook his head. "Sorry, no."

Dominic held out his hand. "I'd like to see the paperwork."

As he read it over, he made a few sounds, then handed it back to the lawyer. "Thank you. I'll contact you tomorrow."

The lawyer retreated from the room before Levi or I had a chance to thank him for coming. Silence once again fell over the room. I wanted to reach into the afterlife and smack both of Levi's parents. They'd given him everything they had but none of what he truly craved.

"Send in Alethea," Dominic demanded.

Although I couldn't see how adding his smug security woman to this situation would help, I didn't say it. All I cared about was Levi and how disappointed he was. I decided to give him a few minutes to process this loss, then suggest we leave.

When the tall redhead walked in, she wasn't smirking or joking. She strode to where we were all seated then stopped and there was compassion in her eyes as she looked us over.

"Alethea," Dominic said, "you investigated Levi's parents. What did you uncover that you think they would have wanted him to know?"

Levi began to unfold to stand. "You don't have to do this."

I pulled him back to the couch. "Levi, give this a chance. You deserve answers. We should at least hear her out."

Chapter Twenty-Eight

Levi

H AD ANYONE ELSE asked me to stay I would have already been gone, but Katie not only knew me as no one else did, but her love for me was undeniable. She was the one who challenged me to never settle for being just good enough or content with surviving. She'd said I deserved answers, but in reality, she did as well.

So I sat back down and thanked Alethea for whatever information she had come across. Considering how our exchanges had gone on the flight, I expected to have to endure some attitude from her as she shared what she knew, but she remained respectfully serious.

"I started my search by retracing the trail Clay Landon had followed. His intel was surprisingly accurate. His report glossed over something that I found puzzling. How did your parents end up working at a nudist resort and why had the owner left it to them when he died?"

I leaned forward, elbows on my knees, and asked, "Do I

want to know?"

She winced. "I thought it was a beautiful story, but I'm not you and have no emotional investment in their decisions."

Sitting back, I met Katie's eyes. She was right, even if it wasn't what I wanted to hear, it was better to know than to spend the rest of my life wondering. "Okay. Tell me everything."

"The owner of the island was related to the young man who was the cause of the car crash that put both of your parents in the hospital. He paid off their medical bills, and at first, it seemed that he was attempting to avoid a civil lawsuit against his nephew. However, according to the hospital staff, he visited your parents many times and became invested in their rehabilitation."

"And my parents used that to swindle him out of his island?" I asked in disgust.

"It's hard to swindle a swindler. His resort didn't just require people to leave their clothing behind. It was like a cult. He sought out people with money and promised them happiness if they left everything behind . . . by behind, he meant to him."

"What was his interest in my parents? They had nothing."

"That question fascinated me as well," Alethea said with an apologetic expression. "So, I dug in. I spoke to so, so, so many naked people . . ." She sighed. "Some of whom have lived on the island for over twenty years. They were there when your parents first arrived. They continued to live there after the original owner died and your parents took over."

"And?" I asked impatiently.

Katie laid her hand on my arm in support.

Alethea continued, "From their statements, I can only conclude that your parents believed in the vision of the island so much that it didn't matter that they had no money. They bought into the idea that a person can reset their life if they're willing to leave everything and everyone from their past behind."

"I see." I did. I didn't like it, but it explained why they'd never contacted me—never even checked in with anyone in Driverton to make sure I was okay. They'd fucking reset their lives and left us all behind. "Thank you. At least now I know."

Seeming uncomfortable in the moment, Alethea inhaled audibly. "I'm sorry they weren't the people you needed them to be. I've been let down by people I cared about." She moved over to stand beside her husband. "But I also know what it's like to be loved by someone who is strong enough to renew my faith in humanity and myself." She smiled at Katie. "You know what that's like as well."

I turned and kissed the top of Katie's head. "I do."

Katie smiled at me with so much love that emotion clogged my throat. I didn't know what I'd done to deserve someone like her, but I was determined to repay her faith in me tenfold.

Holding a finger up in the air, Alethea said, "I realize this isn't what you care about at this moment, but the current value of the island is eighty million dollars. I was able to locate several off-shore investment accounts under the names of both the previous owner as well as your parents and the net value of the estate is close to a quarter of a billion dollars."

My mouth dropped open. Katie's expression mirrored mine. I quickly gave myself a reality check, though. "That money should go back to the people it was taken from."

Alethea shook her head. "Some are no longer around, and my impression was that those who are wouldn't want it back. These aren't young people with the motivation to start over. They chose this lifestyle with the understanding that it would sustain them. In my opinion, the kindest thing you could do for most of them is to let them live out the rest of their lives on that island. I don't know if it's something in the water, but those are some of the happiest people I've ever come across. You could use the dividends from some of the investment accounts to sustain the island and their care."

"They should be given a choice. Also, do they have families who don't know where they are?" I hated the idea of someone out there living with the questions I had.

"Everyone on the island agreed to a no-contact clause, but were allowed to break it as long as they left the island. Very few did."

It didn't seem right to me. "Because they preferred to live naked on an island rather than with their families?"

Alethea raised her hands in a placating gesture. "I'm not claiming to understand them. All I can do is relay what they told me. These were people who weren't happy, for many different reasons, with the world they were living in. They felt isolated and trapped by their wealth, status, situation, or peers. What they were promised was a chance to shed all that and live free of social constraints. That said, the resort is beautiful. They're fed, cared for, comfortable, and surrounded by people who want to live the way they do. Obviously it's your island and you can do what you want with it, but just like you shouldn't shake a bee's nest, I'd let these people be. Or sell the island and let them be someone else's problem."

Half-joking, I nodded toward Dominic. "You want an island?"

"I do collect them." He raised and lowered a shoulder. "It might be possible to corral the current inhabitants to one part of it and do something with the other half. Marc, do we have an undersea bunker off the coast of Florida yet?"

"Not yet," Marc answered.

"This could be the perfect location to install one."

"I'll pull geological specs and look into it."

Dominic met my gaze again. "Give me a week or so to look into what's possible. Then we'll talk."

"A bunker? Do you know something I don't?" I joked.

His laugh wasn't reassuring. "We do live on a spinning ball traveling through space. Marc designs underground bunkers that rival any resort you'll find above ground. They're capable of sustaining small communities for extended periods of time. Originally, I built them for myself and my friends, but now I'm building them worldwide. Having children opened my eyes to caring for future generations as well. Hopefully, we'll never need them, but if an asteroid ever hits or aliens invade, humanity will have a chance to survive."

"Wow." I looked at Katie who seemed to also be attempting to wrap her head around all of this. It didn't feel real. Did that mean it wasn't? "Is this some kind of joke?"

"It would be the least funny prank if it were," Alethea said.

Katie whispered, "I agree."

I turned on the couch and took both of her hands in mine. "Are you okay?"

Eyes wide, Katie murmured, "You're rich, Levi."

"No. *We're* rich."

"Do we want to be?" Her forehead furrowed. "I don't want our lives to change. I mean, yes, I want a ring, and a house and kids, but I love Driverton. I love working at Little Willie's. I don't want to leave that behind."

Never had words hit me deeper or better reflected how I felt. I gripped her hands as I said, "We're not my parents, Katie. We don't have to leave anything behind. If you want, we don't even have to accept my inheritance. If I have you, I already have everything I need."

Wiping tears from her cheeks, Katie said, "I feel the same. Sure, it's nice to dream of being rich, but look at Clay. All he wants is what we've always had—a place to belong. We forget how lucky we are to have Driverton and all the people there who love us. I don't want to end up naked on an island, trying to find a community because we lost sight of that."

I gave her hands a little shake. "I can guarantee you that last part won't happen to us. Naked old people scare me." When that made her smile as I hoped it would, I added, "You know me, Katie. Money has never mattered."

Out of the corner of my eye I caught Alethea shaking her head in wonder.

Katie threw her arms around my neck and between kisses, declared, "I love you so much."

Laughing and holding her tight, I said, "I love you too."

Alethea interjected, "This is why I need to go to Driverton."

"Looks like we're taking a road trip," Marc murmured.

Dominic stood. "It's been a big day for the two of you. There's no need to decide anything today. Bradford arrives tomorrow. If you'd like anyone else flown down, I can arrange that as well."

"How many?" Katie asked, turning in my arms to face him.

"How many what?" Dominic countered.

"People would you fly down?" I wasn't sure where Katie was going with her question until she glanced back at me, and I saw the impish look in her eyes.

"Who are you thinking about inviting?" I asked, already smiling.

Katie fluttered her eyelashes at me. "My parents would love this place. And Aunt Reana won't believe such a house exists if she doesn't see it in person. Ollie will be so jealous if we don't include him. And if he comes Everette should . . ."

Laughing, I said to Dominic, "Save yourself and retract that offer or you'll be flying half the town down."

"We do have twenty-one bedrooms here." He tucked a hand into the pocket of his trousers and said, "Levi, all I ask is that if you think this might be when you propose, tell me so I can fly my wife in as well. She loves things like that."

Katie quickly looked at me, then looked away and I knew there'd be no better time. "Call your wife."

Eyes flying back to meet mine, Katie asked, "Are you sure?"

I kissed her, then, against her lips, growled, "I've never been surer of anything."

When I raised my head, we simply smiled at each other, basking in how good it felt to be together. Then she said, "If we do this, don't forget Clay. His feelings would be hurt if we didn't include him."

"Clay Landon?" Dominic asked.

I nodded. "Do you know him?"

"I know of him." Dominic didn't sound impressed. "Sure. Let him come. It'd be interesting to meet him."

"And the rest?" Marc asked.

"Do it." He waved a hand dismissively in one direction. "Also, invite the Andrades. You know they don't like to miss a good party." He snapped his fingers. "Wait, Bradford's goal was to impress Clay, correct?"

"Sure," I answered, even though that wasn't completely accurate. *Outshine*, not impress. But close enough.

He flexed his hand before him as if deciding how much of his power he wanted to wield. "I could throw an event that would make Clay wonder if he holds any social influence at all."

Katie stood and walked over to him. "Or together we could help Clay feel included in both your world and ours, so he'll stop feeling like he needs to prove himself all the time. If you give him a chance, I think you'd really like him. Clay's goal has never been to make Bradford feel bad. If anything, he keeps trying to win his approval. I'd ask you to help them see past their differences, but I understand that some things aren't possible, even for someone like you."

Dominic's eyes narrowed. "Levi?"

I moved to stand protectively near Katie. "Yes?"

"I met an opinionated woman like yours once."

"Did you?" I hoped this story didn't end with him saying she was resting now on the bottom of the ocean. Could I take down someone like Dominic? Physically, I sure hoped so, considering he was nearly twice my age. Unarmed, could I fend off the amount of security that would intervene on his behalf? That's what I wasn't as sure of.

He knew. He knew exactly how on edge he could put a person without even issuing a direct threat. A smile spread across his face. "I married her, and it was the best decision I ever made. Don't let this one get away or you'll spend the rest of your life wondering who you would have been with her at your side."

I wrapped an arm around Katie's waist. "She's not going anywhere," I said lightly.

Seemingly oblivious to the undercurrent of the conversation, Katie laughed joyfully. "Except home eventually. I'm picturing all of us sitting at Little Willie's talking about this trip and trying to make it not sound like it was something we imagined."

A thought occurred to me then. "You know how you said you love working at Little Willie's? Would you want to own it?"

Her eyes rounded with wonder. "Do you think Ollie would sell it?"

"One hundred percent."

With a huge smile, she hugged me. "Then yes. I'd love that. We could fix it up a little, but not so much that it would lose its character. It could remain the heart of Driverton, a place where people can find help when they need it.

Oh, my God, I'd love that."

"So, it looks like we should accept at least part of my inheritance. We could do some real good with it, both for Driverton and beyond," I said. We could help locals receive better education and opportunities—make sure they kept their homes just like they'd once helped me to. We could also help fund Bradford and Cooper's operation and make it possible to rescue more missing people.

Over Katie's head I met Dominic's gaze. He nodded with approval. What he thought of me and my decisions shouldn't have mattered, but in that moment, he wasn't a wealthy person watching a poor one step into his world. No, he was a seasoned man witnessing a younger one find his footing and his purpose.

Seeing Dominic in that light allowed me to offer with confidence, "Dominic, if you'd ever like a tour of Driverton, we'd love to have you visit."

His smile was genuine. "My family and I would love that."

Chapter Twenty-Nine

Katie

THE NEXT MORNING, I was seated at the mansion's long dining room table with Dominic's daughter, Judy, who'd flown in from college for a few nights, and her teenage brother, Leonardo, who was already working on simultaneously getting college degrees in chemical and aerospace engineering as well as metaphysics. Judy was testing my ability to unlock intricate padlocks while Leonardo was inundating me with questions about life in Driverton.

"There are no police?" he asked.

"Technically, the town falls under the jurisdiction of a neighboring town, but when there is an issue, they always send my brother, who is an acting sheriff, to sort things out. Usually it's about someone's dog getting loose and chasing someone's livestock." As I answered Leonardo, I handed Judy back the padlock I'd opened. She replaced it with a door lock that had an electrical component to it. Luckily, it was a design similar to one I'd come across during an online deep dive about advances in security. I used a technique I'd seen suggested on one of the threads below the video and it unlocked.

"There's no theft in your town?" Leonardo asked.

"Not that I know of. Not from locals. It's difficult to steal anything when everyone knows what everyone else has."

"Try this one," Judy said as she handed me a wooden puzzle box.

I fiddled with it, looking for a place to start as Leonardo asked me, "Do you think there's less crime in Driverton because there is less policing, or do you think that there is less policing in Driverton because there's less crime?"

"I don't know," I said honestly.

"But you feel safe there," he pressed.

"I do."

"Even without security or the police?"

"Yes?" The conversation was taking a turn I wanted to avoid. I called out, "Levi, do you know if my parents have landed yet?"

"Not yet." As if he could read my mind, he joined us at the table. "How's everything going over here?"

Judy leaned forward and stared Levi in the eyes. "What do you think of my Aunt Alethea?"

Levi answered easily. "She's intense."

"She's brilliant," Judy corrected. "If she offers to teach you anything about security systems, run, don't walk to learn from her."

"We'll keep that in mind," I said while shooting Levi a side-eye. Judy was a bit intense as well.

Leonardo looked Levi over. "I saw a photo of you from a year ago. You looked very different."

"Thanks?" Levi said with a smile.

"What kind of training program did you go through?" he asked.

"An informal one via a friend."

"Who?"

"Bradford Wilson."

Leonardo nodded. "Would he train me?" He raised his thin bicep up and flexed it. "I can't stay like this."

Levi chuckled. "You're still growing."

"Up, but not out," he said with a shake of his head. "I need a boot camp or something."

Judy rolled her eyes. "Dad would never let you do that."

Sitting back, Leonardo folded his arms across his chest and said, "Someday, he won't have a choice. I'll do what I want."

Levi took out his phone and even though there wasn't a notification of a message on it, said, "Look at that, Katie, we need to go. We'll have to finish this conversation later."

I slipped away with him to the other room, barely holding back my laughter. "Thank you for saving me."

He pulled me to him and kissed me soundly. "You're very welcome." I stayed in his arms even after the kiss ended, basking in his warmth.

"Hey, Levi?"

"Yes?"

"What do you think our kids will be like?"

He breathed in deeply before answering. "I hope they're the best of both of us."

"Do you think they'll test strangers and interrogate them?"

"Absolutely." He chuckled. "But they'll also grow up knowing that they're loved. They'll be strong, but kind. Successful, but generous. All the things we're striving to be."

I tipped my head back. "You bring out the best in me, Levi. You always have."

"Ditto, Katie. Ditto."

Chapter Thirty

Levi

THE NEXT MORNING was managed chaos. The first to arrive were from Driverton. In an odd tug of war, Clay Landon flew our friends and family down, saying they would be more comfortable traveling with someone they knew.

He wasn't wrong.

When the group arrived, they were dressed exactly as they would have been back in Driverton, but none seemed at all uncomfortable with meeting a butler while dressed in jeans. It probably helped that Clay was similarly attired.

That kindness and endorsement was noted and appreciated by both Levi and me.

To give Dominic credit, his wife was down to earth and didn't bat an eyelash when Mrs. Williams said she'd brought a case of my moonshine for the party. With what appeared to be a genuine smile, Abby Corisi had only asked if moonshine could be served out of regular glasses or if she should order mini mason jars.

Mrs. Williams had taken a moment to weigh the intent behind the question, then had asked if she could help with either getting everyone settled in or with the final details of the party. When Abby smiled and said, "I'll take any and all help you're willing to give," a friendship had been born. Mrs. Williams began to introduce Abby and a reluctant Dominic to everyone from Katie's brother to Adarsh and Manju.

Katie and I introduced her parents to Dominic and Abby ourselves. When Dominic and Abby moved on to meet the others, Katie's mother stepped toward me and took my face between her hands. "You be good to our little girl, Levi."

"I will," I promised.

She released me with a smile.

Katie's father shook my hand. "It took you long enough," he said but there was warmth in his tone.

I hugged Katie to me and kissed the side of her cheek. "I had to get all my stupid out first."

She laughed and shook her head.

Her father and mother exchanged a look that said they agreed with my statement more than they found it amusing. But really, I couldn't blame them and although that would have bothered me in the past, it didn't anymore. My mistakes would always be a part of me, and I was okay with that. They'd help to shape me into who I was.

And who I am isn't all that bad.

It had taken me a long time to come to a place where I could not only think that, but believe it.

The next wave of guests to arrive were Dominic's friends

and there were so many of them that they'd rented out several of the surrounding houses. Businessmen, politicians, royalty and actors. I wondered if anyone said no when an invite from the Corisis was extended. I doubted it.

Ollie, Everette, Cooper and Clay stole me away for part of the day to choose a ring for Katie. Although I was told I could access some of my inheritance funds immediately, it still didn't feel real. Ollie lent me enough money to get a simple diamond. It was beautiful, clear, and exactly what I could imagine Katie wearing every day.

When we returned, guests were gathering in the mansion's ballroom to witness something I'd never imagined I'd do, but that now felt so right. I sought out Katie who was dressed in one of the simple dresses Dominic had given us. It was modest and sexy as hell at the same time. When she smiled at me from across the room, I knew no one could ever tempt me from her side. She was the Yin for my Yang. The apple for my sauce.

I thought of all the times she'd been there for me. How she'd always seemed to understand what I needed before I did. As Alethea had said, I now knew what it was like to be loved by someone strong enough to renew my faith in humanity and myself—and it was damn humbling.

Walking up to her, I cleared my throat and said, "Katie Berber, I shouldn't be nervous to ask you anything. You're my best friend, the one who knows me better than anyone else and loves me anyway. Thank you for believing in me so much that I remembered how to believe in myself. Say you'll marry me so I can spend the rest of my life trying to make you as happy as you make me every time you look at me."

Katie's eyes filled with tears as she held out her hand for me to slip the ring on. It fit her perfectly. The look in her eyes told me I'd chosen well. "I feel like I should have a big, long speech to say as well, but I'm so happy I can't think of anything to say."

"That's a first," Ollie joked before Everette punched him in the arm and reminded him this was serious.

Smiling, Katie looked at them then returned her attention to me. "Of course I'll marry you. I love you, Levi Hale."

"I love you too, Katie soon-to-be Hale."

We laughed and kissed then laughed again.

People came up to congratulate us. Her mother announced she'd always said we'd be perfect for one another, and I let her rewrite that portion of our history. The future held too much promise for me to waste time looking back.

Her brother Tom gave us both long bear hugs. He liked to grumble, but his love for his sister was a beautiful thing to see.

Mrs. Williams told me I could now call her Aunt Reana and that had me hugging her as tightly as Tom had hugged me. Soon afterwards, she wandered off with some of Dominic's friends. I don't think there was a person in attendance who hadn't met her that night and/or received an invitation to stay at her place if they ever wanted to visit Driverton.

Only condition? They needed to do some chores while they were there. Old floorboards didn't mend themselves.

How could they not love her?

Katie and I were congratulated by mailmen and princes that night, dignitaries, and donut shop owners, and none of it felt awkward because everything paled in comparison to how good it felt to know Katie was mine.

Today.

Tomorrow.

Forever.

Chapter Thirty-One

D OMINIC'S HOUSE WAS spilling over with an equal
number of people in jeans and work boots to those in
suits and designer clothing. The group shouldn't have
blended as well as it did, but neither side seemed overly
bothered by the differences in the other.

Bradford had just stepped away from his wife to get her a
drink when Clay appeared at his side. "Nice engagement
party," Clay said. "I couldn't have done better myself."

Bradford's response was a grunt and a nod.

Clay continued, "I had no idea you knew the Corisis."

"What do you want, Clay?"

"A heads-up next time you're considering doing something this stupid."

Rising to his full height, Bradford turned to face Clay.
"I'm in a good mood, Clay. Don't do this."

"No need to get your boxers in a bunch. All I'm saying is
that we may need to be more careful when it comes to this
little competition between you and me."

Bradford's response was a look that said there was no

competition.

"Hey, inviting half of Driverton to a weekend at the Co-risi home was definitely a power move, but . . ."

"But?"

"Do you realize what you've done?"

"*I've* done?" Bradford bit out. His hands fisted at his sides. "I didn't plan this."

"You set the ball in motion for it to happen." When Bradford didn't respond, Clay pressed, "And why? Because I've been helping Ollie?"

"What I do never has and never will have anything to do with you," Bradford ground out.

For a long moment, Clay didn't say anything. The two men stood side by side, looking out over the crowd rather than each other. "Although that's hard to hear, have you considered that if you relaxed a little, we could be friends?"

"I don't like you. Is that what you want to hear, Clay? You're soft, spoiled, and undeserving of the wealth you have. So, no, we couldn't be friends."

Clay inhaled sharply. "I would tell you that I generously overlook how you're ill-mannered and bitter with violent tendencies, but we have bigger issues to discuss. We messed up, Bradford. We stumbled onto a town full of good people without major problems and instead of leaving it as it was, we stayed because we wanted some of that wholesomeness in our lives. This little rivalry between you and me was harmless until we included them. Now, especially after this weekend, people will know about Driverton and our affiliation with it. That makes using it as a base for what you do a whole lot more dangerous for everyone involved."

"I was aware of that issue before this happened." This time Bradford's irritation was directed at himself. "It's why I pushed Levi as hard as I did. He has good instincts and if trouble comes to Driverton, he could hold it off."

"Not alone."

"He won't be."

Rolling back on his heels, Clay said, "Are we going to destroy everything we loved about the town?"

"I sure hope not," Bradford said in a low tone.

"Gentlemen," Dominic Corisi said as he approached. "What has the two of you looking miserable and guilty?"

Neither Bradford nor Clay said anything, both merely shook their heads in response.

Face tightening with impatience, Dominic said, "I don't ask a question twice."

Bradford stood a little straighter in response. Even a brave man knew to be cautious with a coiled rattlesnake. Dominic was someone no intelligent person got on the wrong side of. "We were discussing how involving someone as high-profile as you are might not have been a wise move. Driverton has been able to remain the way it was because it was off everyone's radar. When this hits social media . . ."

"It won't," Dominic said with authority. "I'll make sure of it."

Clay waved a hand. "That's impossible when everyone has a cellphone." All it took was a sustained look from Dominic for Clay to laugh and say, "But I'm sure it won't be a problem."

With a flash of teeth, Dominic said, "This is a happy occasion. Bradford, I've known who you are for a while now. You're the best at what you do and that's gained you as many enemies as fans. I know the feeling. You found my friend's son and brought him back unharmed. That's the kind of thing that can't be repaid with a party. If you need anything to make your operation in Driverton successful, you know how to contact me. You're fighting a worthy battle. No need to fight it alone."

"That's what I've been telling him," Clay said. Both Bradford and Dominic turned to him, but Clay only smiled and continued, "I'm bankrolling an entire underground facility and mentoring people from the town so they'll have enough money to maintain it—"

"Mentoring?" That caught Dominic's attention. "In what?"

"The art of creating wealth."

"Weren't you born with yours?" he asked.

"That's not the point. I know what it takes to make someone successful. I've introduced Ollie to everyone I know and he's soaking up business like he was born to run a company."

Dominic looked around the room. "Which one is Ollie?"

Bradford pointed to where Ollie was laughing with Everette and his wife over something. "He's the one in the blue shirt over there."

"Why choose him to help?" Dominic asked.

Clay rattled off the history of Ollie's family and how they were the glue that kept the town together. When he described Little Willie's policy of feeding everyone regardless of who could pay and how that had led to people in town often donating food to the restaurant, Dominic looked to Bradford for confirmation.

Bradford added, "He's a good man from a good family, but he definitely needed guidance."

"I've been working with him," Clay said. "The only reason he wants to make money is so he can go back and help his friends and family."

"He and Driverton sound too good to be true." Dominic arched an eyebrow. "But I like both of you and what you're trying to do. I'm in."

Bradford looked back and forth between Clay and Dominic. "In? What does that mean?"

"It means we're going to be friends," Dominic said with a smile that made Bradford a little uneasy. "And together we'll find out if Ollie is the man you think he is."

The End

Don't want the story to end? Read on with: Ollie: Driverton 3

Don't miss a release, a sale or a bonus scene. Sign up for my newsletter today.

forms.aweber.com/form/58/1378607658.htm

More books By Ruth Cardello

The Legacy Collection:

The Andrades:

The Barrington Billionaires:

The Westerlys Series:

Corisi Billionaires:

The Lost Corisis:

The Switch Series:

Twin Find Series:

Bachelor Tower Series:

Lone Star Burn Series:

Temptation Series:

About the Author

Ruth Cardello was born the youngest of 11 children in a small city in southern Massachusetts. She spent her young adult years moving as far away as she could from her large extended family. She lived in Boston, Paris, Orlando, New York—then came full circle and moved back to New England. She now happily lives one town over from the one she was born in. For her, family trumped the warmer weather and international scene.

She was an educator for 20 years, the last 11 as a kindergarten teacher. When her school district began cutting jobs, Ruth turned a serious eye toward her second love—writing and has never been happier. When she's not writing, you can find her chasing her children around her small farm, riding her horses, or connecting with her readers online.

Contact Ruth:

Website: RuthCardello.com
Email: RCardello@RuthCardello.com
FaceBook: Author Ruth Cardello
Twitter: @RuthieCardello

Printed in Great Britain
by Amazon